Boss Angel

Boss Angel

Boss Angel

By Joe Broadmeadow and Bobby Walason

Copyright

ISBN: 9798987717424

First Edition: November 2023

Printed in the United States of America by Ingramspark

Published by JEBWizard Publishing, LLC.

Chapter 1 An Unlikely Angel

Gino "The Greek" Suraci pushed his way through the crowd waiting to get into the restaurant, knocking the host to the ground. He only slowed to step over the man as he pushed past the shocked onlookers. The Biltmore Hotel has had its share of drama, but nothing quite like this.

Scanning the room, he spotted the cause of his distress. Meeting the man's eyes, he could see the fear. Good, he thought, the prick needs to fear me.

Ignoring all the stares and murmurs from the crowd, he made his way to the table. Then, without taking his eyes off the object of his rage, he said, "Get lost, sweetheart," to the young woman at the table.

Anthony "the Nose" Arrusso nodded at the woman, and she fled the table, grabbing her wine glass before she left.

"Greek, what can I do for you?"

Suraci leaned down and grabbed the man by the collar. "You listen to me, you prick; you stay outta my fucking business at the port. That's my territory, and I will use you for fucking bait on one of my boats if you keep trying to muscle in." He shoved the man, knocking him back off his chair.

The Nose glared at Gino but did not try to stand. "Gino, is this any way to treat a friend?"

"You ain't no friend. What you are is dead if you fuck with me, capisce?"

Making his way back out of the restaurant, he stuffed a couple of hundred-dollar bills in the pocket of the now standing but terrified host. "Sorry, pal," he muttered, then walked outside like he'd just finished a fine meal.

The next day, Gino sat in his favorite seat at the coffee shop, sipping his Americano. Despite his mother's claim it granted longevity, he'd never developed a taste for strong coffee. All it did for him was keep him awake.

Boss Angel

It never occurred to him to avoid the Biltmore after the shit show the night before. Fuck 'em if they don't like it was his philosophy. His bodyguard had warned him about habits and patterns. He ignored the advice. That's why he'd told them to meet him later. He hated their paranoia. Who'd mess with me?

He paid no attention to the two men using laptops near the fireplace. Just a couple of business guys using the free Wi-Fi as their office.

He also never heard the gunshots.

His next view confused him. He found himself inside an elevator dressed all in white with glorious music playing. When the doors opened, he saw beautiful angels flying, white lights, and an enormous set of pearly gates.

Approaching the gates, he was stopped by a powerful light pushing him back a couple of feet.

"Not so fast, pal, not so fast," said a short but stocky-looking guy in white. "You're on the reject list."

"Who the fuck do you think you are? Reject list? How about I reject your head off your shoulders. Do you know who I am?"

"Yup," the guy answered, tapping his list. "And you are still on the REJECT LIST!. See Ya."

Suddenly, a voice surrounded them, and the little guy bowed away.

"You cannot come past these gates unless you do what I ask. Once this is completed, you may return, and only then will you be allowed into heaven."

"Heaven?" Gino glances around. "This ain't heaven. It's some undigested food or that cheap scotch my idiot brother keeps pouring into the good bottles." He turned and started to walk away. "I'll just wait until I wake up. See ya."

A bright flash of light illuminates a cloud. As the mist clears, Gino sees himself sitting at the table in the Biltmore. As he sips his coffee, the two men using laptops rise from their chairs, guns drawn, and fire.

Boss Angel

Gino sees the rounds striking him in the back and chest. As he watches in disbelief, he knows no one can survive that volume of fire. Stunned, he staggers and turns back to face whatever this place is.

“Wait, I’m really dead? That son-of-a-bitch Arruso had the balls to take me out? Hmm, okay, send me back. I’ll send the prick back in my place. Deal?”

The angel shook his head. “Not how this works, I’m afraid.” He tapped the clipboard in his hand, then pulled off one page. “This is a list of what you must do to be allowed in. Succeed and all will be forgiven, fail and... well, a few bullet holes will be the least of your problems.”

Gino read the first page. “Let me get this straight. I’m dead and can’t enter heaven unless I do this?”

“See, you’re not anywhere near as stupid as this says.” tapping the clipboard in his hand.

Gino glared. “And you’re gonna send me back where I can do things to change the past?”

The angel nodded.

"Wait, who are you anyway? Don't angels have names like Gabriel or something?"

The angel gave a quick look over his shoulder. "You don't want to meet Gabriel. He and the boss had a major fallout over this program," glancing around again, he lowered his voice.

"Last time there was that loud an argument Lucifer and his gang abandoned ship. Trust me, you do not want to get in the middle of that."

"Look, whatever your name is…"

"Achilles."

"What?" Gino said, a bit confused.

"My name is Achilles. Perhaps you've heard of me?"

Gino shook his head. "I don't think so… wait. There was a guy who ran a Greek Pizza Parlor in Providence. He owed the wrong guys some money. They called him the Pizza Angel. Is that you?"

Achilles shook his head. "No, I did not run a pizza parlor. I was a great warrior of Greece and a hero of the Trojan War."

Gino's eyes lit up. "Achilles, of course," he snapped his fingers. "Hey, do you know they named some tendon or something after you? Cost me a couple of grand in a Superbowl game. Damn quarterback had his Achilles whatever all torn up. Had to leave the game.

"Why didn't your mother just toss you in that river and fish you out? Bitch cost me money."

Achilles' eyes flared and he reached for his sword.

"Achilles!" a voice boomed from the clouds. "Put down the sword."

Achilles slid the blade a bit further out, then thought better of it.

Gino, still trying to wrap his head around being dead and all these voices, looked relieved.

"Can I ask you something, Achilles?"

"What?"

"Why do you guy angels wear dresses, carry swords, and have wings? I mean, you can do magic can't you?"

"It's not magic it is the power of heaven."

"And the sword? Why not an AR-15 or a laser gun or something?"

"The sword was the imagination of the artists in the past. We just wear them to make them comfortable."

"But aren't they already dead? What about people like me? I see some guy wearing a dress, carrying a sword, and sprouting wings I ain't thinking angel, I'm thinking hallucinations."

"Enough," Achilles said, holding up his hand. "I was a great Greek warrior who fell in battle. My many great deeds brought me to the attention of the Legion of Angels and I was admitted as such."

"Legion? You guys have a legion hall? Cheap drinks and you all brag about your battle scars and medals?"

Achilles glared. Gino held up his hands in surrender.

"Okay, okay. You were a great warrior turned Angel. So now what? You gonna make me one too?"

"if it were up to me..."

The voice intervened again. "Just tell him what he needs to know and get on with it or I'll send Agamemnon to handle this."

"Okay, okay," Achilles said, then leaned over to Gino. "Agamemnon couldn't even find his way here, let alone handle my job."

"I HEARD THAT." The voice said. "get on with it or your ankle will be the only thing left of you."

Achilles smiled. "He's all talk," then glanced around. "But now onto you. Are you ready to try and rehabilitate yourself? Do some good in the world and avoid the circles of hell?"

Gino thought over his options. There were none. He was dead—or having one helluva nightmare—so there wasn't really a choice. After a moment he answered.

"So send away, the first stop is the. . . ."

Achilles laughed. "You don't get it, do you? We're not sending you back to even the score with the guys who put you here. As a matter of fact, let me give you a little advice, don't even think about it. It won't end well. You have a chance few people get. Especially someone like you.

"Why the big guy chose you, I have no idea. I just follow orders." The angel leaned over to Gino, looking down at him from the platform. "The moment you do anything other than what is asked of you. The instant you decide to return to your old ways and get some vengeance on anyone, you'll find yourself in one of the circles of hell before your next breath... and you won't find it a pleasant experience. Clear?"

Gino stared blankly at the angel before him. He shook his head. "Listen, pal. How the hell am I supposed to do this?"

The angel smiled. "You're a resourceful guy. Figure it out. Remember, the alternative is a permanent change of address to hell."

Gino moved toward the angel, the old habit of hurting whoever got in his way apparently still very much part of his dead persona, but all he found was a handful of nothing.

"Okay, okay. Sorry, old habits. I get it now. So send away, will ya?"

"Remember, follow the list, and you will be forgiven. You can pick someone to help you, but you can only guide them. You have to be the one to change things. You cannot put anyone else at risk. If we see you failing we may, and I emphasize may send you some help. But that was not my decision."

A mist filled the area, and Gino felt himself being pulled down through the clouds.

The angel watched him fade away, then shook his head. Never gonna happen. Guys like him never change. Why do we even bother?

Chapter II Return to Sender

Gino felt a force pulling him back, then fell.

Tumbling through the sky, his only comfort knowing the fall couldn't kill him since he was already dead, he waited for a gentle landing.

Another surprise. Gino learned that death didn't end pain by bouncing off a shed, ricocheting onto a tree, and ending up in a shallow but icy puddle.

He looked to the sky, "You sons-of-bitches ever hear of a parachute for chrissake? Fuckin' angels have wings and they bounce me off the ground." Pulling himself to his feet, he brushed himself off then went looking for the one place he always found comfort and time for thought, a bar.

Getting his bearing, he found himself next to City hall in downtown Providence. At least they sent me someplace familiar, he thought, then headed toward the Biltmore. Kind of ironic he'd revisit the place of his own demise. Few get to do that.

Walking in, few people took notice of him. He found this a bit disconcerting. There was a time when just his walking by a place would spark terror among those who recognized him. It would seem death stole his reputation as well.

The Biltmore was a fixture of downtown. A bit of upscale New York style in gritty, blue-collar Providence. The bar wasn't busy, but it wasn't empty either. The usual collection of barflies—local and travelers—occupied a few seats at the bar or gathered with the fellow solace seekers in booths. They wallowed in the pricey drinks and faux ambiance of success while trying to seduce those lesser mortals who often frequented these places.

Once the place was the residence of the long gone but never forgotten Mayor of Providence, Vincent A. "Buddy" Cianci. A man who personified the lifestyle of the rich and infamous. Buddy was long interred in his grave but the shadow he cast over the city remained.

Gino himself had had dealings with the mayor. Anyone who did business in the city, lawful or otherwise, couldn't avoid it. The mayor had tentacles that reached from the poorer neighborhoods to the upscale East Side. Wise businesspeople played ball buying tickets to fundraisers and other events; wiseguys kept the Mayor on most favored nation status to avoid too much limelight on their activities.

Making his way to the bar, he found a seat against a wall where he could keep an eye on the door. Old habits, even for someone who'd already died, were hard to break.

"What'll you have, sir?" the bartender said.

"Scotch, Johnny Blue, neat."

The bartender's eyebrows arched a bit. "Very good, will you need a menu as well?"

"No, just the drink for now."

By the reaction, Gino got the sense the bartender was wary of pouring the expensive stuff to someone who looked like he'd just fallen from the sky into a puddle. Perceptive prick. Reaching into his pocket, he pulled out a couple of hundred-dollar bills to make the guy relax, not so much because he felt any empathy toward the guy but to keep the drinks coming.

This level of anonymity was unfamiliar yet in some ways comforting. Where once the mere mention of his name, let alone his presence, gave rise to the specter of "notorious mob boss" this lack of recognition gave him time to relax and think.

While there was a time he enjoyed the fearful glances and the sudden departure of people sitting near him, being ignored had its pleasure. He no longer thought of every lingering look or sudden appearance of an unfamiliar face as a threat to his life.

Afterall, he was already dead. He took a strange comfort in that.

Signaling for a refill, he spun on the barstool and looked out the window at the passersby. The recognition came from deep in his subconscious, fighting its way through the fog of his life, and opening up long scabbed-over wounds.

Boss Angel

He barely acknowledged the bartender when the drink arrived, watching as the woman he once thought of as his destiny walked into the bar. She was as he remembered—a bit aged but with grace and dignity—yet her glance conveyed she had no such memory of him.

He debated with himself. Should he call her over? Send over a drink? For one of the few moments in his life he had no idea what to do. In fact, he was afraid. An even more unfamiliar experience.

The span of time, the choices he made, had sent them down different paths and faded the memories.

She walked over to a table where a handsome 60ish gentleman rose, gave her a long kiss, and hugged her closely. The server, apparently familiar with the couple, stood nearby with two glasses of Chardonnay at hand.

He couldn't make out the conversation, but it was clear the woman and her companion with both well-known and well liked.

Turning back to his drink, he tried to stem the flood of memories. Sailing on Narragansett Bay after class at URI. Dinner and drinks at the Spain Restaurant. Those trips skiing in New Hampshire. All of it came flooding back.

He shook his head trying to stop them, but the one he dreaded the most, the one he thought he'd buried all those years ago, came roaring back. The pain was as deep as if he were back in time.

"Gino, you have a choice. No one said you have to follow your father's way. Go to law school or medical school. God knows you're smart enough. Or come with me to Ireland and go to Trinity. You can make your own way."

He didn't need to relive the rest. Sitting here, twenty feet from the one woman he had truly loved. A woman who didn't even recognize him, said it all. He'd made his choice, made his bones in the family, and let her walk away.

If there was anything I would do over, it would be that, he thought, downing the drink and nodding at the bartender.

On his third scotch, he noticed a young woman enter the bar. She bore a striking resemblance, one might say a younger version, to the woman at the table. A moment later, the mystery was solved when she sat down at the table after hugs all around.

Gino watched as she waved off the server. Her mother, he made a calculated guess it was her mother, had a confused look on her face, glancing at her husband.

Within moments, it was plain the conversation had taken a dark turn. Tears formed in both the women's eyes, and they held hands across the table. After a few moments, the husband motioned over the server, handed her a bunch of bills, and the three made their way, arm and arm, out the door.

Gino wanted to run after them. Offer some sort of help. But why? He'd made his choice and had no right to interfere in her life. He felt a helplessness he had never felt before and turned back to let the scotch salve the pain.

"You can't sit here all day," a voice echoed in his ears, "we have things to do."

Gino looked around but saw no one near him. Man, he thought, I can't handle scotch like I used to.

"Listen to me," the voice said, more insistent now. "You know why you're here and reliving old memories isn't one of them. Finish the drink and get going."

"Who the fuck do you..." Gino yelled, spinning in his chair and drawing attention to himself. His head snapping back and forth trying to find the source of the voice.

"Sir, I think you've had enough. Can I call you a ride?" the bartender said, watching for a reaction before he decided what to do next.

"A ride? You little prick, do you know who I am?" Gino stood and glared at the young man. Before he did anything else—his usual throw a punch or point a gun—he noticed the man hadn't flinched. There was no fear, no recognition, not even the slightest motion of retreat. If anything, the bartender looked more amused than alarmed.

“Come on, sir. This last one was on me,” raising the glass then dumping the rest of the drink. Let me get you a ride.”

Finally, the reality of his new world kicked in. He was no longer a feared man. No longer a force to avoid. No longer a threat to anyone. He was a dead man with a past that meant nothing and an uncertain future.

“Nah, sorry, pal. Been a strange day. I’m walking anyway and not far. Sorry.”

“No worries, sir. Come back anytime.”

Gino pushed the money to the well on the bar. “Keep the change, man. See ya.”

Gathering all his strength, he made his way to the door, stumbling only a moment before getting a rhythm to his motion.

Ah, Gino, what have you become?

Chapter III Mission One

Making his way out of the bar, he paused a moment, unsure of where he was supposed to go. Reaching into his pocket, he pulled out the paper the angel gave him. On the top of the list was a date, February 14, 1929.

St. Valentine's Day, he thought, what the hell am I supposed to do about that?

As the recognition of the date bounced around his brain, he suddenly felt cold and found himself standing in a slushy, grimy pile of snow on a dismal sidewalk. Cars blaring their horns raced by and Gino recognized them from history books. 1920's cars battled with pedestrians, horses, and street cars for the right of way. The sun was shining but a cold wind chilled his bones.

Why the hell...he thought, then he knew. This was Chicago, Alphonse "Scarface" Capone territory and he was here to stop the St. Valentine's Day Massacre.

Why the hell would an angel care about a bunch of mugs Scarface decided to rub out? The confusion on his face must have been obvious.

"Can I help ya, pal?" An impossibly young-looking uniform Chicago police officer said, touching Gino on the arm.

Gino looked at the cop and thought, man it is true, when cops and priests start looking young you are definitely getting old.

"What? Oh, thanks officer." Gino said, and what followed he had no idea where it came from. "I'm with the Chicago Tribune and I'm looking for an address, 212 North Clark Street."

The police officer glanced around, then pulled Gino into an alcove. "Why do you want to go there? That's not exactly the safest part of the city."

Again, Gino's mouth was on autopilot. "I, ah, I have some information that something is gonna happen there and my editor wants me to get the story."

"And when is this supposed to happen?" the cop asked.

Gino glanced at his watch. The cop's face scrounged up as he noticed the digital display.

"What kinda watch is that?" he asked.

"Oh, ah, Japanese," Gino answered, jamming his hand into his pocket. "latest invention."

"Hmm," the cop answered, eyes narrowing, and took a step closer. "So, tell me again where you want to go?"

"212 North Clark Street. You think you could point me in the right direction?"

Just then, a uniform patrol car pulled up, and a grey-haired sergeant struggled out of the car, his ass barely squeezed between the door and door jamb. "Dempsey, what the hell are you doin', kid? You shoulda been two blocks further along."

"Sorry, Sarge. I'm just helping this reporter with directions."

"Reporter? For what paper?" the sergeant asked.

"The Tribune," Gino answered. "And your name is?"

"Sergeant O'Malley. Where are you trying to go?"

"Like I told this officer, 212 North Clark. We think something big might happen there."

"Big? The only big thing down there are the rats, some of them with two legs from "Bugs" Moran's gang. So I'd stay away from there. Nothin' good will come of it."

Gino shrugged. "Well, my editor told me to go there, so I have to go."

The sergeant shook his head. "Okay, pal. But I ain't letting you go there alone so the paper can write that Sergeant O'Malley let their reporter get his ass handed to him. So, Dempsey, go with him and don't let nothin' happen to him. Got it?"

"Sure, Sarge. What about the rest of my call boxes? I got three more to pull?"

"I'll cover them. You just make sure this mug doesn't get hisself hurt, got it?"

"Okay, Sarge." He turned to Gino. "Come on, ah... what did you say your name was?"

Sergeant O'Malley rolled his eyes. "Try not to get yourself killed either, kid. I hate all the paperwork." He stuffed himself back into the car and drove off.

Gino chuckled. "My name is Gino. Gino ah Brown. Sorry you got stuck with me."

"Don't be. This is better than dodging dogshit on the sidewalk and pulling callboxes all day. Let's go." He pointed down an alley. "I know a shortcut."

Chapter IV Trying Not to Get Killed

Making their way through the alley, they dodged overflowing garbage cans and the occasional rat, some the size of small dogs.

"Christ," Gino said, "what do they feed those rats? They're fucking enormous."

Officer Dempsey paused a moment, giving Gino the hairy eye-ball. "You've never seen a rat before? How long have you lived in this city?"

"Ah, a couple of years. But I usually avoid alleys like this."

Dempsey shrugged, kicked at a rather bold rat sniffing at the garbage on his shoe, and dragged Gino out of the ally onto the street. He pointed toward a large warehouse at the end of the block. "That's North Clark. The number you want is another block down the street. Let's go."

Gino hesitated a moment, trying to come up with a way to warn the cop he needed to be careful without giving away his secret.

"Listen, Dempsey. I should tell you my boss hates me and he has some connections to the wiseguys in town. I wouldn't be surprised if he sent me here into the middle of some gang turf war. He wouldn't shed a tear if I got caught in the crossfire. Be careful."

Dempsey chuckled. "Don't worry, if anything happens to you I'd have to answer O'Malley, and I ain't doin' that. Come on, it's Valentines Day. What could happen?"

Walking down the street, they turned onto North Clark. Parked just up ahead was a marked police car. "Look," Dempsey said, "I bet O'Malley came here to keep an eye on me."

"Wait," Gino said, grabbing the cop by the arm. "That's not O'Malley."

Dempsey pushed him away, then took a step toward him. “Listen pal, you put a hand on me again and I’ll give you a private tour of our lockup. Got it?”

Gino put up his hands in a gesture of compliance. “Sorry, kid. I just have a bad feeling about this, okay? I don’t trust my editor and I don’t like the looks of that police car. Something ain’t right.”

Dempsey stared at Gino for a moment, then turned back toward the police car. He started to walk toward it, when he noticed two guys dressed in suits come from out of a side alley. They looked like detectives but… it took a moment for him to see the Thompson submachine guns held close their side.

“What the fuck,” he muttered, pushing Gino back into the alley. “They ain’t no cops, something is wrong here.” He glanced around, spotting a variety store at the other end of the street.

“Listen, you run down there and call the station. Tell ‘em an officer needs assistance and give them the address.” He drew his weapon. "I'll keep an eye on them until the cavalry gets here." He pushed Gino toward the store. "Run!"

Gino hesitated a moment. Is this what I'm supposed to do? What if this kid gets himself killed? Unsure of what to do, he started to run, pausing just a moment to say, "Don't be a hero, kid. Moran and his mugs ain't worth dying over."

As he ran toward the store, he heard Dempsey say, "Bugs Moran? How do you know…" but the voice faded in the distance.

Chapter V One Off the List

Gino rushed into the store, startling the old couple behind the counter. “You got a phone here?” he shouted.

The shocked couple raised their hands and backed away, the old gent pointing one finger at the phone behind the counter.

Gino grabbed the phone. “What’s the number for the cops?” he said, holding the receiver just away from his ear and his other hand poised over the rotary dial.

The woman took a step forward. “Here, let me dial it for you,” spinning the dial then taking a step back. “I remember it since we’ve been robbed a few times.”

Gino smile at the woman, trying to reassure her he was harmless.

“Chicago Police Department, Sergeant Jackson.”

“Hi, ah, yeah, listen one of your cops, Officer Dempsey, needs help. He’s at 212 North Clark and there are guys disguised as cops with guns there. Get him some help, now!”

“Hold on one minute,” the sergeant said. Gino could hear muffled voices. “Okay, I got some cars on the way. What’s your name?”

“It doesn’t matter who I am, just don’t let that kid get killed.” Gino slammed the phone down, then looked at the terrified couple. He took a twenty out of his wallet and threw it on the counter. “Thanks for the phone. You may want to stay inside for a bit.” Gino smiled then ran back out the door.

Off in the distance he heard sirens drawing closer. He started back down the street, then saw Dempsey holding the two guys in suits at gunpoint. The police car was nowhere to be seen. As he drew closer, one of the guys in a suit spun around an opened fire.

“No!,” Gino yelled. “Look out, Dempsey…” As the words came out of his mouth he was jerked from behind.

Mists surrounded him, blinding him. Several moments went by and he found himself in another part of the city.

Looking around he had no idea where he was. A couple of feet away was a newsstand. He walked over and saw a copy of the Chicago Tribune. The date was September 15, 1929.

The headline read.

Hero Cop Prevents Mob Hit

Grabbing the paper, he read the story.

"Late yesterday morning Patrolman Christopher Dempsey interrupted an attempted hit on Bugs Moran. The officer managed to apprehend two armed men by himself, killing one, despite being wounded in the attack.

"Shortly after the incident, an abandoned car, made up to look like a Chicago Police car, was recovered partially burned along the lakefront. Inside were sawed-off shotguns and fake police uniforms.

"Chief of Police William Russell praised the actions of the young officer and recommended him for a Medal of Valor, the highest award issued by the Chicago Police Department and a meritorious promotion to Detective."

Good for you, kid. Good for you, Gino thought as he slowly faded away finding himself back at the bar at the Biltmore.

"Would you like a scotch, sir?"

Gino smiled. "Yes I would," glancing around at the four or five others at the bar. "Give the bar a round on me."

"Yes sir!" the bartender smiled. "Having a good day, sir?" as he started pouring the drinks.

"I am now," Gino smiled. "I am now."

Chapter VI Next

Gino sipped the scotch, glancing at the door every once in a while looking for her. He knew it wasn't likely to happen, but then again he never thought he'd be dead and changing history either, so there's that.

"She's not coming back," a somewhat familiar voice said from behind.

Gino turned and saw the Angel who'd been there when Achilles sent him back sipping a gin and tonic.

"You angels drink?"

The guy smiled. "Of course we do. Why do you think they call it heaven?" downing the drink and motioning for another. "It's on my friend here," he smiled.

Gino nodded at the bartender.

"So, like I said, she's not coming back. That was a door you slammed shut years ago. And even if she did, she'd just think you were crazy. By now she's seen the story of your exit from the planet, at least your first exit, and she wouldn't recognize you anyway."

"Thanks, that makes me feel so much better." Gino sipped the scotch, then turned to face the angel. "You got a name? Or do I just keep calling you angel?"

"Joseph Benjamin Paul," he replied, tipping the glass toward Gino.

"What kind of name is that for an angel?"

"Well, Gabriele and Michael taken and my parents liked the sound."

"So Paul is you last name?"

The angel stared for a moment. "No, it is Schwartz, but it causes too much confusion so I shortened it. Just call me JB, it's simpler that way."

Gino studied the guy. In any other world he'd be a guy at the bar nobody would notice. They'd never give him a second look. Maybe that was part of the magic, hiding in plain sight.

"You know, I've always wondered about something concerning angels," Gino said.

"What's that" JB answered, trying to figure out how to get the bartenders attention.

"Well, aside from the fact I didn't think you guys even existed, I always wondered why all those old paintings and statutes of angels show them wearing skirts and carrying swords.

"I mean, why does an immortal creature need a weapon? Wouldn't just standing there and letting some Roman gladiator slash and stab you with no results be enough to scare 'em to death?

"As to the skirt, you and Achilles in dresses would look like someone with an identity crisis and no fashion sense."

"That's an easy answer."

"Oh yeah, what then?"

"Angels didn't paint the paintings of sculpt the statutes, that was human imagination. Angels are designed to be present and unobtrusive. There when you need us."

Gino looked at JB for a long moment. "Have you looked around the world recently? If there was ever a time we needed angels it would be now. Are you guys on strike or something?"

JB put his hand on Gino's. "Did you ever wonder maybe it would be worse if we weren't here?"

Gino thought about that, then caught the smirk on JB's face.

"Just kidding. I follow my instructions and interfering with life is a last resort. You guys do have free will you know."

Gino shrugged and went back to his drink. "So I suppose you're here to send me on my next adventure."

“Actually, I am coming along for the ride,” he said, draining the glass. “I always wanted to see Las Vegas. You might want to finish that.”

Gino put the glass to his lips, downing the drink. “Listen, can you try for a softer landing this time. Last time you handled my travel arrangements it was a less than pleasant experience.”

JB smiled, waved a hand over his head, and they vanished from the bar.

Chapter VII LA Not LV

As the mist faded, Gino felt the warm California sunshine on his face. Looking around the crashing waves of the Pacific caught his eye.

"Ah, JB, not to be critical here but you missed Vegas by a couple of hundred miles. This is Los Angeles."

"I'm starting to understand why they picked you for this gig. Quite observant aren't we?" He reached over, pulling the list from Gino's pocket and smacking it against his chest.

"Read the second entry on the list."

Gino grabbed the paper and glanced at it. "Bugsy Siegel."

"Great, and he can read as well. And where did Siegel get whacked?"

"Beverly Hills."

"And thus I give you," waving his hand toward the city and away from the beach. "The road to Beverly Hills."

Gino shook his head, closing his eyes for a moment. "And how are we supposed to get there, walk?"

JB was nowhere to be seen. Gino started to look for a cab when a limo pulled up. The driver's door opened and a fully chauffeur-uniformed JB came around and opened the door for him.

"Your carriage, my liege lord."

Gino smiled, then climbed into the car. "I'm starting to like this."

JB chuckled. "Enjoy the moment, I'm about to deliver to you to meet with the guys who are looking to hire someone to kill Siegel."

"What? How the hell am I suppose stop the killing by meeting them?. If I refuse they'll just go find someone else."

JB shrugged. "True, but on a positive note they can't kill you right?"

Gino just shook his head.

"Look, this is all part of the deal. That's why the big guy picked you. You'll figure it out."

Turning down an alley, the car came to a stop at an abandoned warehouse.

Gino put the window down and looked around. "Why do these mugs always think meeting in places like this is smart. If I wanted to meet with someone, we did it in a nice bar or restaurant and acted like civilized people, not rats scurrying from the light."

"Where you discussed killing people, right? Like all civilized people do?" JB said, looking at him through the rearview mirror.

"Yeah, well it was better than these dumps. Wait here and let me see what's up."

Gino stepped from the car and walked by the driver's door. JB was on a cell phone looking at Las Vegas Hotels on Expedia.

"Hey, how can that thing work we're in 1947?"

JB smiled, pointing finger to his chest and mouthing the word "Angel." Gino rolled his eyes and continued on

Making his way to a door half hanging off the hinges, he pulled it the rest of the way open. As he started in the door, a flock of pigeons flew past forcing him back.

"Jesus Christ," he yelled, wiping pigeon shit off his suit.

"He can't help you," JB yelled from the car.

Gino glared at the angel, then made his way inside. Light filtered through broken skylights and pigeon feathers floated in the air. Gino heard the sound of two people talking, muffled but distinct, from a partially lit back room.

He walked a few steps closer, then called out "Hey, get out here." Gino didn't believe in niceties, he preferred controlling the situation. Make them come to him.

Two men appeared from the room, one tall and lanky, the other a meatball with arms and legs and no neck. The tall one held a briefcase. Both armed. Years of looking for threats had taught Gino to notice such things. Too bad he missed that last one, he wouldn't be in this mess in the first place.

One of the guys took a step closer. "We hear you do renovations."

Gino gave the man a scowl. "What are you guys? Hollywood producers? Dispense with the theatrics. Tell me who and where and let me deal with the rest."

The men exchanged glances, then the guy with the brief case opened it. Inside was a disassembled sniper rifle, two photos, one of Bugsy and one of his girlfriend, Virginia Hill, and a map.

Gino took the photos, tossing the woman's photo back at the men. "I don't do broads unless they're shooting at me. You want her taken out, you do it."

"But the boss said both."

Gino paused a moment, cocking his head. "Are you deaf, or just stupid? I said I don't do broads." Tapping the photo or Siegel. "This guy's is good as dead. She is your problem."

Gino took the briefcase, handing Siegel's picture back to the guy. "I don't need this."

"Don't you want it to be sure?"

Gino took a step toward the men. "No. I never forget a face. If I want to kill somebody I always remember what they look like." He glanced between the two men. "Now where's the money?"

"You get that when the job is done."

Gino slammed the case shut and tossed it to the floor. "See ya, boys. Not how I work," and headed to the door.

"Wait," the taller of the men said. "It's not here, but it is close."

Gino glanced at his watch, making sure the men didn't see the digital display. "One hour, what's the closest bar?

And not some shithole, someplace you guys have probably never been."

The tall guy chuckled. "Real smart ass, aren't you?"

"Yeah," Gino said, turning to face the man. "And very good at what I do."

The meatball spoke up. "Ocean Vista Lounge, couple of miles down along the beach. We'll be there in an hour or so."

"Good," Gino sneered, retrieving the briefcase. "The tab will be on you."

Chapter VIII Now What

"So?" JB said as Gino got in the car.

"Well, good news, Dad, I got the job. They're bringing the money to some joint on the beach, Ocean something..."

"Ocean Vista, great food and drinks." JB said, pulling a U-turn and heading out of the lot. He could see Gino's face and the raised eyebrows in the mirror. "I wasn't always an angel you know. I used to be a lounge singer."

"Of course you were," Gino said, settling back in the seat.

"Wanna hear some Sinatra?"

"Not unless you wanna die again. Just drive."

Ten minutes later, they pulled into the lot.

"You wait here. Keep an eye on things," Gino said, stepping out of the car. As he got to the door, a hand came around and opened it for him. JB, now attired in a suit a blind man would find offensive, stood smiling behind him.

Gino glanced toward the lot, but the limo was gone. "I thought I told you to stay in the car."

"You did," JB smiled, pushing past him. "But that doesn't mean I would listen to you. Oh look, seats at the bar with an ocean view and a view of the door, not that you're very good at that safety trick. First round is on you."

As they settled in at the bar, Gino tried to come up with an idea to stop the killing. "Look, JB, playing the bad guy here comes naturally. They'll buy the whole act, but after I get the money then what? They ain't gonna wait forever to see this guy whacked."

"What is it they really want? Why do they want to take the guy out?"

"Money, it's always about the money. They think he and the girlfriend were skimming off the construction money, which I'm sure they were. I would. Couple of million if I remember right."

"So get them to give back the money." JB said, staring out the window at the beach bunnies sunning themselves.

Gino put his hand on his head. "I'm surprised you lived long enough to make it to puberty. Guys like me don't give money back. You either kill us and take it or we kill you and keep it."

JB turned back to look at Gino. "Well, then. Seems to me you have only one choice. Convince them you didn't take the money."

Gino shook his head. "Did I say puberty? I meant past your first year. How can somebody be so stupid? Which part of this aren't you…" Gino stopped mid-sentence.

"What?" JB asked. "Did you think of something?"

"Maybe. Give me a minute to think it through."

"No time," JB nodded toward the door. "Your new friends are here."

Chapter IX A Plan On the Run

The two wise guys spotted Gino at the bar. Gino named them Laurel and Hardy since they weren't much more than a couple of comedians in the wrong business.

Laurel and Hardy sauntered over and sat at seats to the right and left of Gino. JB had made himself scarce. But this was a poor attempt at intimidation.

"So you got my money?"

"Yeah, but not in here. We gotta take a ride."

Gino glanced between the two men. "Barkeep, you got a pen a paper I can borrow?" The confused look on Laurel and Hardy's faces made it all the more enjoyable.

The bartender handed him a pad. Gino started to write, then looked up. "You guys can read, right?"

"Listen, pal," Laurel said. "I'm done with your smartass altitude."

"Yeah, right," Gino said, holding up one finger in the universal sign of shut the fuck up. He finished scribbling, then showed the paper to the two mugs.

No rides, no nothing. Bring the money here or get out.

Switching between the two men, he saw they were trying to figure out their next move.

"Hey, Gino," JB said, appearing from nowhere. He was now dressed in a snazzy suit complete with a fedora and topcoat. Stylish, but a bit out of place for California weather. He looked once over each shoulder then pulled back the front of the topcoat. Protruding from inside was the butt stock of a Thompson Sub-machine gun.

Hardy's eyes grew three times larger than normal. Laurel raised his hands in a mock surrender. "Look, we're just following orders. We'll tell the boss what you said. It's not our call, okay."

The pleading tone of his voice said it all. Gino wouldn't be surprised if they had to go change their shorts.

"Thanks, JB," Gino said, ignoring the men. "Sit down and finish your drink. Our friends are just leaving."

In a scene reminiscent of their namesakes, Laurel and Hardy made a hasty comedic exit out the door and fled the jurisdiction.

JB sat down and motioned for two more drinks. "Was that part of the plan?"

"Not sure, I am kinda winging it here. Nice suit by the way if it was January and we were in Chicago. You might want to change it before anyone notices."

Gino glanced around the bar to see I anyone had noticed, then turned back. JB now sat in the chicest of Hollywood beach attire.

"Christ, JB, somebody's will definitely notice that."

"I told you before, we do not read Christ in on this project and people only see what I let them see. Now where the hell are those drinks? Ah never mind." JB climbed up onto the bar, danced all the way past the bartender mixing martinis for other patrons, grabbed the Scotch bottle and filled their drinks.

"Hmm," Gino said, "there's a talent worth having. But don't you think he'll notice the bottle sitting here?" he tilted his head at the bar.

As the words came out of his mouth, the bottle floated back to its spot on the back top shelf.

"Why didn't you do that in the first place?" Gino asked.

"I always wanted to dance on a bar, they frowned on it in Harvard Divinity School."

"You went to Harv... ah, never mind. Just let me think."

Thirty minutes later, Laurel came back in, alone.

"You got the money?" Gino asked.

"Yeah, yeah. It's here. And so is the boss. He's outside and wants to talk to you."

"I told ya, I ain't going nowhere."

"Just, just in the parking lot. You and him, alone. He's standing out there now with the money. Nobody's goin' anywhere." He glanced at JB; a bit taken aback by the wardrobe change. "Take him. Your, ah, assistant and his heater with you."

Gino took a long drink, keeping his eye on Laurel, then put the glass down. "JB, you stay here with our friend. If you hear any gunshots outside, shoot him."

JB started to object, then thought better of it. He wasn't shooting anybody, but Laurel here didn't know that. "You got it, buddy. We'll be right here when you get back, and at least one of us will be alive."

Gino chuckled at the B-movie mobster impression, then walked out the door.

As Gino walked out the door, he spotted a familiar face standing in the parking lot next to a Lincoln. Someone was inside the car, it looked like a woman but with these guys you never knew.

“How are ya, Jack?”

The confusion on the guy’s face said it all. “Do I know you?” he asked.

“No, but I know you,” Gino said. “Jack Dragna. Since when do bosses handle their own contract negotiations?”

“Since you insisted on the money coming to you. If the Havana guys hadn’t given this to me as a direct order, I’d have just blown that fuckin’ restaurant up with you in it and been done with this nonsense.”

Gino ran a quick history lesson in his mind. Dragna headed the LA family and he was known to hate Siegel. The Havana guys was an infamous meeting of all the mob bosses in the US where they reorganized things into “La Cosa Nostra” “this thing of ours” and formed what became known as “The Commission” to resolve disputes.

Siegel had the unfortunate luck of being the first "problem" they needed to resolve. And they decided to solve it by permanently terminating him.

"Okay, Jack. I will take care of the problem soon as you hand over the money."

Without taking his eyes off Gino, Jack raised a finger, waving it toward the car. Gino took a step to the right, putting Jack between him and the car just in case guns came out.

To his surprise, a young woman stepped from the car carrying a briefcase. She walked over, put it on the ground, then opened it, revealing stacks of 100s.

"Wanna count it, sweetie?" she asked.

Gino shook his head. "Nope, I know where to find you if it comes up short."

She closed the case, put it at Gino's feet, then leaned into whisper in his ear. "If you want help spending it, call me," she smiled and walked away.

Jack waited for her to get back in the car. “Listen to me. You do this job and I may have some other work for you.” He started back to the car, then stopped. “But there is one thing.”

“What’s that?” Jack asked.

“Don’t even think about calling my daughter. That would be a mistake.”

Gino smiled. The thought had never crossed his mind.

Chapter X Decisions

Back inside the at the bar, Gino put the briefcase on the floor leaning against the bar, one foot propped on the top.

"So what's the plan, boss?" JB mumbled, in his best gravelly-throated mobster impression.

"Will you stop that." Gino said, "You sound like a hungover nitwit."

"Not what I was going for," JB answered. "So what are you going to do?"

"Can I just kill Dragna?" Gino said, sipping his drink.

"What do you think? A bit incompatible with your goals, isn't it? If we just needed someone to kill off the problem we have a whole bullpen of the world's best killers on ice in the seventh circle."

"Seventh circle?" Gino said.

"Don't tell me you never read Dante's Inferno."

"Oh, that circle. Yeah I read it but apparently the simplest solution is not the answer."

"There you go, Occam." JB said, signaling for two more drinks.

"Occam? Ah never mind. Let me think here."

JB turned and looked out the window, watching the surfers, sunbathers, and waves.

"I always wanted to try surfing; you know." JB said, breaking the silence. "See a different perspective on life."

"What? Will you…" Gino stopped mid-sentence.

JB looked at him, studying the far-off stare on Gino's face. He could almost hear the man's brain churning ideas.

"A different perspective, That's it." Gino said, coming out of his reverie.

"How so?" JB said.

"Look, these guys live in a world where they trust no one. They don't even trust their own families. They think everyone is trying to take something from them. It blinds them to other possibilities.

"All I have to do is prove to Dragna, and those guys on the commission, that Bugsy Siegel isn't stealing from them. He's using the money he skimmed off the top to invest in a more lucrative business model. Something even better than casinos when it comes to cash flow."

"And what would that be?" JB said.

"Politics," Gino said. "Buying the services of Senators and Congressmen to get access to the public till."

"Really? This is something that valuable?"

"Don't you read the papers? Almost every person elected to office, Congress in particular, comes out much richer than when they went in. They use insider trading, and awarding contracts to companies who kickback money to them, lining their pockets while pretending to do the people's business."

Gino slapped JB on the back. “This will work out perfect and nobody has to die.”

“And how, exactly, are you going to get Siegel to part with the money he stole to fund this adventure? Let alone convince Dragna and the others to go along with it.”

“First, I figure out which politician to target then I convince Siegel there is money to be made here. After that, we just show the commission how much money they can make from it and all’s right in the world.

“And there’s a name, I just can’t place it yet, of a guy who will go on to become pretty famous as a Senator. I just can’t put my finger on it. But it will come to me.”

Gino sat in silence, wracking his brain for the name.

“McCarthy!” Gino said, snapping his fingers. “Joe McCarthy, he’s running for Senate in Wisconsin.”

“Wisconsin?” JB said, “that’s a bit of a stretch from here, no?”

"Yeah, but the money is still green there and politicians don't care where they get the money to run. Believe me, from what I remember about this guy having him in your pocket will pay dividends for decades."

Gino downed his drink, threw a couple of hundreds on the bar, they motioned for JB to follow him. "I need you to be chauffeur JB again. We have to go visit Siegel."

"But I've been drinking. I can't drive."

"Well then fly us there. I don't care how you do it just do..."

The last of his words were lost as they both disappeared into thin air.

Chapter XI An Investment with No Risk

Gino and JB stood just outside the house Siegel shared with Virginia Hill. The two had a reputation for violence so the approach had to be a cautious one. Of course, being dead limited the worry of personal harm, so there was that. But gunshots in this upscale neighborhood might draw some unwanted attention.

"So what are you gonna do, knock on the door and say I'm here to kill you but you could give money to this guy you never heard of and you'll be okay."

Gino smiled. "Yup, something like that. You keep forgetting I have, or had, a long history in the mob. I know names and the things they did. Come to think of it, maybe that's why I got picked for this job.

"Siegel is a business guy above all else. This whole Vegas thing was visionary for a mobster. I'm gonna tell him, Joe

Vallone sent us. Vallone ran the Milwaukee family back then, it was part of the Chicago Outfit. Bugsy will know the name."

"But is a name enough?" JB said. "You think this guy's gonna invite us in cuz you know a few names?"

Gino smiled. "No worries, I have an invitation," reaching into his pocket and showing the Model 1911 .45 pistol to JB.

"Hey, you know the rules. No violence. Give me that," JB said, snatching the gun away.

"I ain't gonna shoot him. Just use it if he won't let us in. Now give it here and let's go." He put his hand out.

JB hesitated a moment then smiled. "Wait, let me be the, what did you guys call it, the muscle. Yeah, I'll be the muscle and show him the gun if we need to."

"You're enjoying this aren't you?" Gino said, walking up the long drive to the front of the house.

"What do you think? I don't get to do anything close to this on most days and my most days number in the thousands."

Approaching the front door, Gino paused. "Okay, let me do the talking. And no stupid impressions. Just try to look ah, intimidating as best you can."

Gino's look didn't instill confidence in JB but he nodded. "Strong and silent it is."

Gino stood on the landing at the door. "No matter what happens, just follow my lead."

"You got it, boss... ah, I mean Gino." JB shrugged.

Ringing the bell, Gino took one step to the side to make anyone looking out the peephole struggle to see.

The door swung open and Bugsy Siegel stood there. He was a handsome bastard, despite the cigarette dangling from his lips. Giving Gino and JB the once over, he slipped a hand inside his pocket.

"What do you mugs want?"

Gino put his hands up and to the side. "Just to talk, We got a proposal from Joe Vallone."

"Vallone, why didn't he just pick up a phone and call me?"

Gino shrugged. "I don't get to ask Mr. Vallone those questions. I just do what I'm told. Call him if you like."

Siegel waited a moment, then took a step back. "So propose to me."

"Can we come inside? I don't want any eyes on us while we talk." Gino said.

"Sure but keep your hands where I can see them and that goes for the gorilla too." nodding at JB.

Gino looked back and swore he could see a bit of a smile cross JB's face. "Look you can pat me down if you want. My associate can stay outside if that makes you more comfortable."

A voice from behind Siegel broke the tension. Virginia Hill stepped into view toting a Thompson Submachine gun. "You sneeze in our direction and I'll blast you into tomorrow."

Well, that would be a step toward my actual former life, Gino thought, but kept it to himself. The he heard JB say, "Be right outside if you need me, Boss. You know, to claim your remains and take them home."

Gino now stood alone with Siegel and the gun-toting girlfriend.

"You were about to propose," Siegel said, a sarcastic smile crossing his face.

"Okay," Gino said, "but let me finish the complete story before anybody jumps to conclusions."

Siegel nodded and Hill titled the barrel down, keeping her finger on the trigger.

Gino stepped inside and closed the door. "Can I put my hands down now?"

"Sure, why not?" Siegel said. "You can even propose on one knee if it makes you feel better."

Hill chuckled.

"Listen, the commission thinks you're ripping them off with these cost overruns. They are not happy."

Gino noticed the quick glance between Siegel and Hill.

"They gave Dragna the contract to take you out."

"And you're it?" Siegel said as Hill raised the barrel.

"Nope, not exactly, but I'm here to offer you an out. One that works to everyone's benefit."

"Nothing works to everyone's benefit. Somebody always comes out on top with more money."

"But in this case, you and machine gun Virginia here both live to enjoy a long and profitable life."

Siegel eyed Gino for a long moment. "And how does this work? What does Vallone want from me?"

"An investment." Gino said, relaxing a bit as Hill again lowered the gun.

"An investment in what?"

"Not what, who," Gino answered.

"Okay, I'll bite. Who?"

"A guy running for Senate. Name of Joe McCarthy. We pump money into his campaign he takes the heat off your projects in Vegas and you can show the commission the wisdom of your using the money for things more beneficial and less offensive to them than lining your pockets."

Siegel waffled a bit, struggling with the complexities of the offer and the fact that this guy just showed up out of the blue. Hill was more vocal.

"Bugsy, he's trying to get us to cop to stealing the money so the commission can justify whacking us. He's probably the guy they sent to whack us, just looking to gain our trust." She started to raise the barrel once again. "Let me just blast this guy and his cohort will shit himself as he runs away."

The gun suddenly flew out of Hill's hands and she fell into Bugsy, knocking them both to the ground. JB stood above them, huge smile on his face and the machine gun now firmly in friendly hands.

"Want me to plug them, boss?" he said, unable to resist doing the voice.

"No, no," Gino said. "Let's give our hosts a chance to reconsider."

An hour later, Bugsy and Hill were firmly convinced of the wisdom of the offer. Gino and JB headed out the door.

Back on the sidewalk, JB grabbed Gino by the shoulder. "Okay, now that those two want to play what do we do about Dragna and the commission?"

"This is business, JB. They wanted to whack Siegel because it would be better for their business if they weren't getting ripped off. This solves that problem and gives them another source of money. Not to mention a powerful friend to keep the Justice Department from sniffing around Vegas."

"How's that?" JB asked.

"This McCarthy guy. He's some kind of crusader nutcase. He'll turn the country upside down looking for enemies of the United States and leave the wiseguys alone."

JB let that digest for a moment. "Ever hear of the law of unintended consequences?"

Gino shook his head.

"You might want to consider learning about it if you want to succeed in these matters. They sent you to prevent bad incidents from happening, not create worse ones."

Gino shrugged. "One problem at a time, my friend. One problem at a time."

Chapter XII Greed Conquers All

"Jack," Gino said, putting his hand out as the mobster stepped from the car. "How are you?"

"Is he dead?" Dragna growled, taking a long drag on his cigar.

"Let's just say I have a better offer for you."

Dragna handed the cigar to Laurel who was standing just behind him. "I paid you for one thing and one thing only. So if Siegel ain't dead, you will be shortly and I'll get someone who knows what they're doing."

"Jack, Jack, listen to me. Siegel was skimming chump change. It wouldn't even be a rounding error with the opportunity I'm offering you and the commission."

Dragna turned to Laurel as Hardy climbed out of the car to join them. "Do you believe this fucking guy? He thinks he can negotiate with me and the commission." Turning back to face Gino, he smiled.

"Okay, pal. Here's your choice. I get my money back and you die quickly or you die slowly and I get my money. But either way I get my money."

"Jack, you're missing a very important point."

"What's that?"

Gino tilted his head toward the car. Sitting in the front seat, next to Dragna's daughter, was JB. The two were laughing and smiling and the daughter waved.

"My friend there likes your daughter. Would never want anything to happen to her. But, if something were to happen to me... well that might change.

"Why don't we go inside, just you and me, and I'll explain how not killing me is a better way to get a lot more than the money in that briefcase you gave me. Once you hear the story, you can inform the commission. I'll bet they'll see this as a mutually beneficial change of plan."

Twenty minutes later, Dragna and Gino appeared from the restaurant. JB was now outside the car, standing next to Dragna's daughter who was leaning out the window.

They were both still laughing.

Dragna looked around for the bodyguards. Then he heard muffled voices from the trunk. He glared at JB, who shrugged.

"They started getting feisty, so I had to, ah, contain them."

Dragna shook his head, then turned to shake Gino's hand. "I'll give you one thing, pal. You got some stones on you. But if half of what you say is true, we're gonna make a bundle of dough. I'll be in touch."

Dragna walked to the driver's side and climbed in.

"Aren't you gonna let Laurel and Hardy out of the trunk?"

Dragna smiled. "Nah, a long hot ride in there might teach'em a lesson. Or I may just whack'em myself. I haven't decided.” Gunning the motor, he rocked the car back and forth as he flew out of the parking lot.

Gino waited for the car to leave, then punched JB in the shoulder.

“Hey, what’s that for? There must be some rule about hitting an angel.”

“You locked them in the trunk? What did Dragna’s daughter see? Are you insane?”

“Marie.”

“What?”

“Her name is Marie and she will have no memory of what happened. But, once I verify my rules of engagement down here, I may see about taking her to dinner. Can’t be an angel all the time you know.”

“You set one foot near that woman and I will kill you myself.”

"Hard to do since I am already dead. But have at it if you like."

"Arrrgh," Gino yelled, then headed back inside. "Come on, my guess is we will have an answer pretty quickly. Greed conquers all."

Chapter XIII One Last Obstacle

"Hey, is there a Gino here?" the bartender said, holding his hand over the receiver.

"Right here," Gino answered.

"Grab the extension at the end of the bar," the bartender said, waiting for Gino to pick up before he hung up at his end.

"Speak," Gino said, ignoring the pleasantries.

"Gino, Jack. You got a deal But our associates want to told about everything, if you get my point."

"Oh, I do. I certainly do. I'll be in touch." He hung up the phone.

Making his way back to his seat, he finished the drink. "Okay, we are all in agreement."

"Well, that's not entirely true," JB said.

"What do ya mean?"

"Hmm, let me think. You've got everybody to agree to a deal with Vallone in Milwaukee to fund this Senator wannabe, which is admirable don't get me wrong, but you've left out one important part."

"What's that?" Gino said.

"Vallone doesn't have a clue about any of this."

"That is a good point but think about this for a minute. Why do you think all these mugs agreed to this? I mean, we show up out of the blue yet these guys, who trust no one, are falling over themselves to work this deal with us. Why is that?"

JB sat for a few moments, staring out the window. Then, the light went on. "Greed. It's all about greed, right?"

"You know, for an angel you're not that dumb. Show 'em the money and these guys will line up like little kids at a candy store, trust me. Vallone is no different."

JB slid off the chair. "Let's go, then. We need to get this done."

"Can I finish my..." As the words trailed off, Gino felt himself flying through darkness. Mere moments passed and he found himself standing on Jefferson Street near the river in Milwaukee. JB was nowhere to be seen.

At least I landed on my feet this time, Gino thought.

Glancing around Gino looked to the sky, "Couldn't you at least let me finish my drink?"

A cab pulled up; the off-duty sign illuminated. The horn blared at Gino, startling him. Gino started to give him the one-finger salute, then recognized the smile. Jumping in the cab, Gino said, "You know, I don't know how you died but I willing to bet someone killed you."

"Nonsense, I died from old age in a Diocesan Nursing Facility at 102 years old."

"Really?" Gino said, eyebrows rising to the middle of his forehead.

"Nah. Someone did kill me in 1941. I never got his name."

"Too bad, I'd send him a thank-you card. But I want to know the story."

JB paused a moment to pull out into traffic. "It doesn't matter. Ancient history."

"Come on, I want to know." Gino said, leaning forward over the front seat, his arm on JB's shoulder.

"Pearl Harbor. The USS Arizona. I was there on temporary duty as a fill in for the base Chaplin."

Gino slumped back in his seat. "Wow. I mean, I would never have guessed."

"Why's that?" JB asked. "Don't I seem the Chaplin type?"

"No, it all makes sense with you being an angel and all. Why can't we go back there and get you off the ship before it happens?"

JB remained silent for a long time. "Because I wouldn't consider doing such a thing unless I could save them all. And even if I could, remember what I said about the law of unintended consequences?"

"Yeah. What of it?"

"if I saved them all, there'd be a shortage of angels right now."

That stunned Gino into silence. He just stared out the window and wondered how much of history, and death, is just bad luck.

Fifteen minutes went by then JB pulled the cab to the curb in front of a grocery store.

"Where are we?" Gino asked.

"Vallone's business and residence is right across the street at the next intersection. He keeps an office for his real job in the back of the grocery store. The problem is, there is only one way in. There are always bodyguards of the Neanderthal-type itching to pull limbs of would-be assassins. And guys with heavy artillery of the machine gun variety nearby.

"Since Vallone's faction is part of the Chicago Outfit, he worries about getting taken out as part of a power struggle. Thus, the high security."

Gino blinked a few times. "And you know this how?"

"Come on, I work for a boss who is omniscient."

"Well if he knows everything, why doesn't he find a way to stop this?"

"The Prime Directive," JB answered, as if everyone knew that.

"What?"

"The Prime Directive. Didn't you ever watch Star Trek?"

"Wait, the rules of heaven come from Star Trek?"

JB laughed out loud. "No, no, Rodenberry had a dream about the Star Trek concept and in the dream my boss inserted the idea of a Prime Directive." JB suddenly sat up straight, tilted his chin, and in a serious and official sounding voice said,

"... the right of each sentient species to live in accordance with its normal cultural evolution is considered sacred, no one may interfere with the normal and healthy development of life and culture...

"My boss set things in motion and then took a purely hands off approach. With the exception of the '69 Mets and New Coke he stuck to the policy."

"New Coke?"

"Yeah," JB chuckled, "He let the kid take the lead on that one. It reinforced the need to stick to the Prime Directive... tive... tive... tive."

Gino shook his head and stepped from the car.

JB rolled down the window. "Wait, don't we need a plan?"

"Why start now?" Gino said. "Park the car and meet me in front of the store. I have an idea."

Gino studied the comings and goings. To the uninitiated, it looked like just any old Mom & Pop market. But to guys like Gino, the unmistakable signs of a mob front were obvious.

So was the FBI surveillance vehicle parked across the way. Marked like a telephone company truck, the two "workers" seemed less interested in the dangling wires and more intent on taking pictures of people entering and leaving. Especially those guys who went in, stayed just a few moments, and left without any groceries.

JB ducked under Gino's arm to peak around the corner.

"What are you doing?" JB said.

"Aren't we on a stake-out?"

"Christ, no..."

"I told you he..."

"Yeah, yeah." Gino said, pushing JB away. "Let me ask you something, do the rules allow for a little property damage and minor injuries?"

"What kind of injuries?"

"Nothing permanent. Maybe a bruise or two. At worse a broken bone."

"I suppose we can accept that. What are you going to do?"

Gino smiled. "Not me, you."

"Me? Do what?"

Gino turned JB around and pointed to the FBI team. "You see that telephone company truck?"

"Yeah."

"Well they ain't telephone workers. That, my friend, is an FBI surveillance team. Your gonna take your cab and ram the truck so those guys on the ladder get knocked off."

JB looked between Gino, the truck, and back at Gino.

"I don't know about this. This might not go over well with the big guy."

"Look, your boss obviously thinks stopping the Siegel hit is worth some risk. This is a dangerous business. A little bump or broken bone seems a small price to pay. Besides, can't you soften the blow a bit with your angel magic?"

"Yeah, I guess."

"Besides, you said he's omniscient right? Wouldn't he already know what I am planning to do?"

JB frowned. "Oh don't start with the George Carlin routine about god making a rock so heavy he can't pick it up. That was good for a laugh but it's not how things work?"

"So he can't make a rock that heavy?" Gino smiled.

"Forget it. Just tell me what you want me to do."

Gino waited until he saw the cab heading toward the truck. He knew the noise would draw everyone's attention, at least for a moment or two. He'd use that moment to slip inside the store then figure out how to convince the bodyguards to see Vallone once he was inside.

The sound of crunching metal and shouts brought him back to reality. JB had misjudged the speed a bit, afraid to do any real damage, and the two agents were just clinging to the ladder. Perhaps it was better in the long run.

He took a moment to watch the circus as one agent scrambled upside down along the backside of the ladder, then took off after the now fleeing JB. For a moment Gino was tempted to watch what happened but then thought better of it.

He ran to the front entrance, walked past the cash registers, and spotted one gorilla occupying a seat which seemed to have been swallowed by his enormous ass.

Slowing his pace so as not to alarm the beast, he stopped a few feet from the man.

"I'm here to see Mr. Vallone. I'm from Havana."

The man lumbered to his feet, rising to over 6'8" tall. "What part of Milwaukee is dat?"

Oh boy, Gino thought, another one whose shoe size exceeds his IQ. "if you just tell Mr. Vallone what I said, I'm sure he will want to see me. And if you don't, when he finds out I was here and you wouldn't let me in, well… I wouldn't want to know what he'll do."

This caused the guy's limited intellectual ability to short circuit. Torn between his instinct to dismember Gino and his at least basic understanding that something more complex was afoot, he vacillated between choices..

"Wait right dere," he said. The fear of the boss overcoming his natural instincts to hurt somebody.

Meanwhile, sirens screamed on the street and a Fire Rescue truck arrived along with the cops. Gino wondered how long JB let the agents chase him before he kicked in the angel overdrive.

A moment passed and two more gorillas arrived. The original one and someone he apparently considered more intellectually suited to evaluate the situation.

"Grab the wall, pal," said monster number two. "Once Vito pats you down we'll see what Mr. Vallone wants us to do with you."

After the thorough and unnecessarily rough search for weapons, more a smack down than a pat down, monster number one spun Gino around and held one of his giant paws against his chest, pinning him to the wall.

Gino heard a door open, and Vallone appeared in the hall. Looking Gino over for a bit, he motioned for the bodyguards to take him into the office. Pushing him into a chair, they took up positions on either side while Vallone returned to his desk.

"So, you're from Havana they tell me. Why should I believe that?"

Gino smiled. "Look, if you're not interested in making money, I'll leave. The commission sent me to make you an offer, a part in some action bigger than you can imagine. But, if you're not willing to hear me out, so be it." Gino started to rise but was less than delicately slammed back into the seat.

"Hey, no need to be unpleasant here boys," Gino said, looking between the two monsters. He turned back to face Vallone. "You don't pay them by the pound, do you? Must cost a fortune."

"You know what, smart ass. Here's what I'm gonna do. I'm gonna make a call. And if what they tell me is the least bit different from what you claim, I'm gonna let Vito and JT do whatever they like with you, capisce?"

Gino tried to hold his reaction, he didn't want to give anything away, but a call might prove to be a problem.

Vallone reached for the phone.

"Look, call whoever you want but you may not want to use that phone."

Vallone held the receiver to his shoulder for a moment. "Why's that?"

"You hear those sirens outside? They're because my associate and I interrupted an FBI surveillance team that was watching your place here. I'm sure they're listening on the phones as well."

"What are you talking about, pal?"

"Send one of your boys here to check it out. One monster should be enough to keep me in line."

Vallone motioned with his head, a one gorilla lumbered out the door.

Deciding to use the opportunity to spread some fear, uncertainty, and doubt, Gino leaned forward in the chair. This got a bit of a reaction from the bodyguard, but Gino froze in place.

"Not doing anything buddy, just wanna talk to your boss," Gino said. "Look, I'm starting to think you pal in Chicago, Sam Ginancana, kept my little visit a secret. He probably figured you'd just take me out, like you seem intent to do, and then turn you over to the commission. You get whacked and he gets a bigger piece of this action."

"Why the fuck should I listen to some mutt off the street. Sam would never double cross me. We go way back. Just sit there and shut your mouth or I will put a hole in your head right there."

Gino shrugged, sitting back in the chair but he could see the doubt creeping into the thought process. These guys don't believe anything except that everyone is playing their own angle.

A minute later, man mountain one came lumbering back inside. He tossed an FBI identification card on the desk, then looked at Gino. "How d'ya pull dat off?"

Vallone picked up the ID. "Where'd you get this?"

"Our friend Sgt. Malone is out there. He snatched it offa da guy in the meat wagon. Guy got knocked out cold when he fell off the ladder. Ya shoulda seen the shitshow out dere."

Vallone took the ID and stuck it in his desk drawer. "Okay, pal. Whaddya say your name was?"

"I didn't. Nobody gave me a chance," Gino smiled. "Gino, Gino Suraci from Providence. I'm with Buccola's crew."

"Yeah, I know Phil. So tell me what this scam is all about."

An hour later, greed had worked its magic once again.

Chapter XIV The Root of All Evil

Cop cars raced around looking for the guy who'd try to kill two FBI agents. The streets were crawling with uniform cops and plainclothes detectives. It looked like someone had stepped on an ant colony, except it was a cop colony now intent on exacting some street justice.

"So explain to me why this works again," JB said, sipping his beer in a dingy downtown bar. He couldn't help watching and smiling a bit at the havoc he'd unleashed.

Gino looked up from his drink. "He who is greedy for gain troubles his own house, But he who hates bribes will live."

JB's eyes grew wide. "A killer who can quote the bible, I'm impressed. Did you actually read it or was that on some billboard you came across?"

"My mother. She kept one and read it daily."

"A habit you never acquired?"

"What do you think?" Gino said, downing his drink and motioning for another. "Just before she died, I went to visit her in the hospital. I'd just gotten out of my first bid in the can. She took my hand, looked me in the eye and quoted that passage." He paused, turning away and wiping something from his eyes.

"It was the last thing she ever said to me."

JB put his arm around Gino. "I'm sorry, my friend."

"Yeah, well. It was a long time ago." Pulling away from JB's hand on his shoulder.

They sat in silence for a few moments, then Gino leaned back in his seat. "Okay, so now we need to put this whole thing in motion. We take the briefcase with the money Dragna gave me for the hit and deliver it to the campaign headquarters of this mutt running for the Senate."

"But he's not a crook," JB said. "What makes you think he'd accept money from guys like you."

Gino broke into uncontrollable laughter. It took him a few minutes to regain control. "JB, for a guy who works for a place that supposedly knows everything about everybody you are shockingly naïve.

"Politicians make us guys look like those old geezers waiting to die gathering change and small bills in the Sunday mass collection basket. We walk in with a case full of money, we'll have to make sure we count our fingers when we leave.

"The problem is not getting them to take the money. The problem is getting them to follow through with the promises they make when they *see* the money. These guys and money are like a teenager trying to get his first piece and promising to love the girl after. Not very likely."

JB looked at Gino for a bit. "First piece of what?"

Gino stared at the floor shaking his head. "Never mind, JB, never mind. Finish the drink and let's take a walk."

Chapter XV Dominoes

Gino and JB stood outside a small, non-descript office building. Along the sidewalk leading to the front were signs promoting the campaign of Joseph McCarthy for the U.S. Senate.

"Kind of a dull place for a campaign headquarters, don't ya think?" JB said.

Gino smiled. "Well, my friend," holding out the briefcase, "let's go see what, or who, our money can buy."

"Wait, we're just gonna walk in, show them the money, and say here, it's yours as long as you leave the mob alone to do what they want in Las Vegas?"

"Well, something like that," Gino winked, walking toward the door and muttering under his breath, "and show him how the alternative means an early grave instead of a seat in Congress."

"I heard that," JB said. "You know the rules, no violence. No old Gino. Nobody gets killed."

Gino shrugged, then held the door for JB. "But they don't have to know that do they? Listen JB, the best way to persuade people isn't to kill them, it's making them believe you *will* kill them. Simple as that."

"May I help you?" a young woman asked. She wore a McCarthy for Senate button and had an infectious smile. She was a walking billboard for innocence and naivete`.

"We're here to see Mr. McCarthy," Gino said, trying to exude charm.

"Do you have an appointment?" the woman asked.

"Well, no," Gino answered, "but we'd like to discuss… "

JB interrupted, his voice dark and ominous. "Listen, sister, you just skedaddle in the back there and tell Mr. McCarthy that if he wants to win this election, he'd best get out here… now!"

The woman stood frozen, eyes blinking in rapid succession, uncertain what to do.

"Well?" JB said, taking a step toward her.

That brought her out of her shock and she fled toward the back office.

"What the hell was that?" Gino said, backhanding JB on the chest.

"Hedging my bet. The head guy said you can't revert to your old ways," JB paused a moment. "But they never said anything about me." He smiled.

Gino shook his head. "I thought lawyers didn't get into heaven."

JB smiled. "Most don't, but every once in a while we a let few in just in case we need 'em. I pay attention."

A few moments later, the woman returned with a bespectacled man in a suit way too big for his frame, tie askew, and a stack of forms in his hand.

"How can I help you gentlemen? My name is George Samson. I'm the campaign manager for Mr. McCarthy."

JB and Gino exchanged glances.

"Nice to meet you, Mr. Samson," Gino said, "My associate and I…"

"George," the man interrupted. "Please call me George."

"George, then," Gino replied. "Is there somewhere we can discuss things in private?" glancing at the young woman.

"Anything you have to say, you can say in front of Marie."

Gino took a small step toward the man, lowering his voice. "Mr. Vallone sent us."

Th man's eyes grew two sizes larger and he shot a glance around the room. "I see, well, ah. That will be all, Marie. I will handle this from here."

Marie nodded, the look on her face gave away her relief at not having to be involved.

"Let's step into my office, shall we?" George said, gesturing toward the back of the room.

Once they were all seated, George said," Can I get you anything? Coffee, water?"

"Nah," Gino said. "This won't take long." He put the briefcase on the desk, spun it so the opening faced George then pulled the cover back.

If George's eyes widened at the mention of Vallone, they bulged from their sockets at the sight of all the money. "You, ah, you want to make a donation to the campaign?"

Gino leaned over the desk. "We want to buy the campaign and all its assets, if you get my drift."

George leaned back in his chair. "Mr. McCarthy is not for sale. He's a man of integrity. A man of honor. A man of… "

"Yeah, yeah. Stop with the campaign speech. Maybe I chose my words wrong. We want to, shall we say, aid Mr.

McCarthy in winning the election in exchange for some small concessions."

Gino then laid out the conditions. George listened with great interest, occasionally glancing at the money. When Gino finished, George sat in silence for a moment.

"I think... let me rephrase that. I know Mr. McCarthy will be amenable to helping any businessman who wishes to bring jobs and prosperity to American cities. And while Las Vegas may not be in the future senator's district, he can certainly appreciate the benefit to the country. I think he will readily agree." He reached for the briefcase.

Gino slammed the cover, nearly separating George from three of the fingers of his left hand.

"If you don't mind," Gino said, his eyes narrowing, "we'd like to hear it from Mr. McCarthy himself.

George, beginning to sweat a bit, smiled. "Let me assure you I speak for Mr. McCarthy and anything... "

Gino held up one hand, pulling the case closer to him. "Unless Mr. McCarthy has lost his voice and writes the note himself in front of us, we are leaving and the money comes with us."

George left the office, returning two minutes later with the smiling candidate for senate, Joseph McCarthy, and another man.. He walked right over to Gino and put out his hand. Gino stood and shook his hand.

"Nice to mee you, ah, George didn't mention your name."

"That's because I didn't tell him," Gino said. "Who we are is unimportant. Who we represent is. Did George mention that?"

McCarthy glanced at George. "He did as a matter of fact and he explained your proposal. Let me just say that anything I can do to foster successful business endeavors in the country is a priority for my campaign and will be my focus when elected." He paused a moment and looked Gino in the eye. "But I am not for sale, sir. If I accept this money, I will do everything I can to support your cause as long as it comports with the law and with the rules of the office."

The man who'd come in with McCarthy remained silent. Gino walked over to him. "And what is your function?"

The man smiled. "I am an, ah, adviser to Joe. Just making sure he stays within the law."

"Ah, another lawyer. Whatever, but the conditions stay. He agrees or we walk with the money." Gino thought the man looked familiar, something within his memory. He just couldn't place him.

"Let me get this straight. You want me to be helpful to our friends in Las Vegas, right?"

"That's it. Just keep their interests in mind whenever the Senate decides to do something that may be, shall we say, incompatible with their business plan."

McCarthy paused a moment, wheels turning. He looked at the other man. "Dick, what do you think?"

The man nodded once yet said nothing. Leaving the room.

“Okay, Mr., ah, what do I call you?” McCarthy said.

“Let’s just say I’m an angel investor and leave it at that,” Gino closed the case and slid it across the table. “We’ll be paying attention to things over the years. I hope there’ll be no need for us to visit you again.”

McCarthy cleared his throat. “No, I understand our arrangement and rest assured our friends in Las Vegas will have a strong voice for them in Washington. Of course, I will have to focus my attention on something. I’ve made it a promise in my campaign to weed out undesirables.”

Gino held the man’s stare for a moment. “Here’s a thought. Why not go after all the commies infiltrating our country? Them Russians are sneaky bastards.”

McCarthy nodded, letting the thought percolate a bit. “You may have something there, my friend. I will consider it.”

Gino nodded at JB and they left the room. As he passed Marie's desk he winked and waved. She didn't return either.

Outside, JB had to run to keep up with Gino. He seemed not to notice JB's looking at him as they walked.

"Something bothering you, Gino?"

"Yeah, that other guy in the room. I know the face but just can't place it."

JB shrugged. "He seemed okay to me. Nothing tricky there."

"That's it," Gino said, grabbing JB by the arm. "That guy was Dick, ah, Richard Nixon. Tricky Dick Nixon. He's a future president and a future disaster."

"Well, that's not our problem is it? He's not on the list," JB said. "And I wanted to ask you, why tell him to chase communists? How many can there be?"

Gino stopped mid-stride. "You really don't pay attention to things that go on down here, do you?"

Chapter XVI No Good Deed

As Gino and JB left the office, a large Lincoln Continental limousine pulled to the curb in front of them. The driver got out, came around to the passenger side, and opened the back door.

"Gentlemen, if you would," he said, motioning for them to get in.

"I don't think so, pal. Who the hell sent you?" Gino growled, bending a bit to get a look in the back seat. He couldn't quite make out the face, but the barrel of the .45 pointed at him told him all he needed to know.

JB leaned over to Gino. "Where's the harm," he whispered, "not like then can kill us."

Gino smiled. "Good point," and climbed into the car.

They rode in silence for a few minutes, then JB said, "Hey, ah, Mr. Gunman, I get motion sickness facing backwards. Can I switch seats? Otherwise we're gonna have to take the car to the carwash." He held is hand over his mouth and mimicked puking.

"You puke and I'll shoot you."

"Okay, suit yourself, but that will just add blood and guts to the mess." JB turned away and winked at Gino. When the gunman lowered the weapon a bit, Gino made a guttural sound then lunged across the seat stripping the gun from the man's hands.

Pointing the gun at the kidnapper turned victim he asked, "Now, who sent you."

"Let's just say I'm from Chicago and they don't like people using them to muscle in on business." Tilting his chin toward the gun, he added, "Where we're going that .45 is going to be seriously outgunned."

Gino reached over and took the gun, tossing it back to the man. "Put it away before you get hurt. I'll take my chances with the commission."

Ten minutes later, they pulled into an underground parking lot. The car came to a stop and the door opened.

Two men stood waiting at the door. Gino pegged one for the muscle, his name wasn't important. But the other guy was unmistakable. A little younger looking than the pictures Gino remembered, but there was no doubt in his mind who this was.

His diminutive stature, glasses, and sharp suit gave him the look of a businessman or accountant, not the feared mob boss of the Chicago Outfit he would soon become.

Sam Giancana stood silently, arms folded, and waited for Gino and JB to get out of the car.

"Sam, can I call you Sam? How are you?" Gino said, projecting an air of confidence that was more pretense than reality.

"Who the fuck are you two and who sent you?" Giancana scowled. "Nobody comes in without our say so. You give me one good reason why I shouldn't have my boys here plant you in the nearest dump?"

Gino raised his hands. "Look, Sam, I don't know why Joe Batters didn't fill you in, Ask him. We just came to do a job and move on. If there's a problem here, it ain't with us."

The mention of Joe Batters, aka Tony Accardo, the boss of the Outfit, got a reaction out of Giancana, but he tried to hide it.

"There's no way Batters sent you here without telling me. You mugs are dead." The two men with him pulled out their weapons.

"Look," Gino said, "call the guy. Tell him what I told you. If he trusts you like you think he does, he'll vouch for us. And if not, well, you might take us out. But if what I say is the truth and you don't call, then the problem will be yours."

Gino could see the uncertainty wreaking havoc in Giancana's brain. If there is one common trait every wise guy in the world shares its paranoia. Trust gets you killed in this business. Treachery gets you more money.

"Where are you from?" Giancana said after a moment of indecision.

"Providence," Gino answered. "I work for Buccola."

There was the slightest of indications in Giancana demeanor as the tension eased. The fear, uncertainty, and doubt Gino planted worked their magic. Giancana pulled one of the men closer, whispering in his ear.

"Listen, my guys will take you back wherever you need to go," taking a step toward Gino. "Meanwhile, I'll check with Providence and Batters. If they tell me this is legit, no harm done. But if not, I will find you wherever you are and it will not be pleasant, capisce?"

"Tell you what, Sam," Gino said, closing the distance. "Why don't we just wait here and then you won't have to find me?"

If paranoia is the one thing wise guys suffer from then someone showing no fear is the one thing they universally admire. They put too much stock in their ability to intimidate.

Most people are afraid of dying. Someone willing to risk it. Someone that has the balls to provoke it is to be admired.

The ploy worked. Giancana walked away. The first gunman motioned toward the car.

"Thanks, pal. But we'll walk from here. Nothing personal, but I don't care for people who point guns at me."

"But Mr. Giancana said…"

"And I said, no thanks. You wanna shoot us in the back while we walk away, have at it. But I'm not sure that will sit well with the boss."

Once again, paranoia took hold. The man returned to the car while Gino and JB headed toward the street.

As they left the building, JB grabbed Gino's arm. "What was all that stuff about Joe Batters? Who's he?"

"He's the boss of the Outfit, for the time being. Sammy there well soon take over. I just spread a little doubt in his mind. These guys trust no one. He couldn't afford to do anything that might derail his rise. He knew if he called the boss no matter what he said he wouldn't trust it.

"He had no idea who sent us or what they kept from him and no way to find out. I took a gamble on his need for self-preservation. Besides, not like they can really kill us, right?"

JB remained silent.

"Right?" Gino said, pulling JB toward him.

"Yeah, yeah. They can't kill us. But I may have forgot to mention that you might feel it a bit."

"What?"

"Well, technically you are alive," making the air quote signs. "You technically would die again. Of course, I'd bring you right back but there would be a bit of, what is it doctor's say, discomfit."

"Jesus, JB, you might have wanted to mention that."

"Jesus isn't..."

“Gino held up his hands, “Yeah, yeah I know. Not read in on this. So now what? We’ve done all we can to stop Bugsy from getting drilled. Where do we go from here….” His voice trailed off as the fog enveloped them.

Chapter XVII Unintended Consequences

Once again, JB's magic deposited them into a bar. This one in Washington DC. Out of the window was a spectacular view of the US Capitol Building. The bartender took their drink order and hurried off to make them.

"So why DC?" Gino asked. "If our next target is that mob," pointing to the capitol, "where gonna need a lot more than you and I."

"Just watch and learn. You have to understand nothing happens in a vacuum. Everything affects everything else."

Just then, horns blaring and the shouts from bullhorns drew Gino's attention to the street. A crowd, led by a pickup truck covered in American flags, marched toward the US Capitol. The bore signs reading, "Get the Commies out of Hollywood" and "The Reds are Back in Hollywood" and other slogans.

"What that hell is that all about?" Gino said, grabbing his drink from the bartender.

"That is what you put in motion with McCarthy. Remember what you said? You told him to go after the commies. He did. It's tearing the country apart. Didn't you ever read history? You always accuse me of ignorance?"

"Well, yeah, I'd read about it. But I didn't know it was this bad."

Gino looked back out as the crowd surged past.

"Finish your drink, I have one more thing to show you."

The two left the bar and wandered down the street, stopping in front of the library.

"What's this?" Gino asked.

"A library, haven't ever been to one before?"

"Well, no to be honest."

"On my Lord," JB said, "Come on."

They went into the archive section. JB spoke to the librarian's research assistant who left for a few minutes, returning with several old newspapers. One was dated June 22, 1947.

JB thumbed through a few pages, then laid it out on the table. He pointed to an article.

Gino looked down and saw the headline. "Wise Guy Casino Investor Gunned Down in LA."

Gino finished reading, then looked at JB. "They killed him anyway. Those sons-a-bitches. I told you this play nice wouldn't work. If you want to stop a guy from killing someone else, you kill him first. What we should do is... " He stopped mid-sentence.

"Wait, I failed here. Am I getting... "

A voice startled them both. "You're not going anywhere."

Gino looked to face the most stunning woman he had ever seen.

"Who are you?" Gino said.

"This is Maggie," JB said with a sigh. "She's my boss."

"Wait, women are bosses in heaven?"

"Yup," JB said. "My guess is she's here to tell me all the things I did wrong. You know, just like when we were really alive."

Maggie took a step forward, and JB flinched.

"JB, I'm here to compliment you on teaching our little project here alternative methods of dealing with problems. To be fair, we gave you this task with little hope anything might change. You actually accomplished more than we expected."

Maggie made a quick, almost imperceptible motion with her hand and they found themselves in a bar near the White House. She flashed a sign to the bartender for drinks.

"And now it's time for a change of plan."

"And this means I'm heading back?" JB said, dropping onto a bar stool. "But I was just starting to enjoy this."

"We noticed," Maggie frowned. "The stunt with the FBI agents was not exactly protocol."

"True," JB smiled. "But it worked."

"Well, while that may be true it changes nothing. You are relieved of your assignment here and can return. If we need you again, you'll be notified."

JB downed the drink then stood. Turning to Gino he said, "Look, I know you can't change what you were, but you can change others. Keep at it, my friend. I can see something in you that you may not see in yourself."

Gino shook his hand but kept looking at Maggie. He leaned into JB. "Listen, ah, are there any rules about, well, you know," motioning his head toward Maggie.

JB shook his head. "Rules, no. But I wouldn't try it. She didn't become head rehabilitation management boss for nothing. It wouldn't end well for you."

Gino smiled. "We'll see about that."

And with a nod of his head, JB vanished leaving Gino alone with Maggie.

Motioning for another drink, Maggie raised a finger calling Gino to come closer. "Just so you know, there are no rules except mine. Do one thing I don't like. Try anything I don't explicitly tell you to do. And you will regret it. What's the word you use? Capisce?"

Gino nodded and settled onto the seat. *We'll see about that, lady. We'll see.*

Chapter XVIII More Than One Way

Gino slid his stool closer to Maggie, turning to face her. He leaned in, putting his elbow on the bar and resting his chin in his hand.

"So sweetheart, what do you want me to do to, ah, for you."

At first there was no reaction, then she tilted her head slightly glancing sideways at him for a moment. Turning away, she took a long gulp of her drink.

"First, if you call me sweetheart again you will lose the ability to speak. Use your imagination on how I will do that. Second, if that line ever worked on anyone they must have suffered from some serious mental defect.

"And lastly, I don't like you. I don't like your type. I don't like that we have to waste time on you when there are so many other more deserving people. And I really don't like how you look at me as a challenge to lure into bed."

She leaned in closer. "Try anything remotely like that again and you will lose your ability to enjoy any such amorous activity. I think you can guess what that will entail." She extended her hand and made a motion like cutting with scissors.

Gino held up his hands. "Okay, okay. Can't blame me for trying." As he turned back to face the bar he thought, *you watch what I can do, sweetheart, you're not the toughest one I ever won over with my charm. I'll have you screaming my name.*

Maggie smiled, still looking straight ahead. "You haven't quite got the concept of angels, do you?"

"What's the supposed to mean?" Gino said.

She looked at him once more, the grin turning into a scowl. "You may not think I'm the toughest challenge in your sexual conquests... but I'm likely the only one who can hear your thoughts. Understand? Or should I ask the bartender for a pair of scissors? Snip, snip."

She finished her drink and motioned for another. "And I wouldn't be the one screaming, you would."

Oh shit, Gino thought, *oh shit.*

"Okay, I'm sorry, all business from this point forward. But can I ask one question?"

"Okay, just one," Maggie sighed, taking a seat at the bar.

"Why Maggie? Is it short for Margaret? That was my grandmother's name."

"No, it is short for Magdalene. A very popular name where I come from."

"So you were a 'working girl' like here?" Gino asked.

Maggie shook her head. "That entire story is a bunch of bullshit. Mary Magdalene wasn't a hooker. She was one of the smartest of those around Jesus. Kept him in line. The others didn't like it and let the rumor spread after his death. It is a name of great honor and I bear it proudly.

"But Maggie is easier and most people just assume it is short for Margaret. Satisfied? Now let's talk about how we're not gonna fail on this next task."

"So, I get another chance?" Gino asked, a bit cowed, yet intrigued, from the previous conversation.

"That's way over my pay grade. My job is to work with you while JB goes back to discuss things. What decision they ultimately make is not my concern. But I'd try to take advantage of this moment if I were you."

Gino nodded. "Okay, what do we have to do?"

"I'm not as familiar with you mob guys as JB was so I'll need you to help me with the personalities and relationships but we are going to stop the killing of a guy named Sam Giancana."

"Giancana?" Gino said, "the CIA killed him. Everybody knows that."

"What's the CIA?"

"What's the…?" Gino rolled his eyes. "You know, this belief us mere mortals have in angels being omniscient is way off the mark. Why do they send someone like you if you don't even know the basic story?"

Maggie smiled. "I'll let you in on a secret. This free will thing has some defects. We can't stop people from doing all sorts of crazy shit. So this is the best solution. Try and go back and fix what we couldn't anticipate.

"I'm starting to understand the thought process on why we use guys like you."

"I'll take that as a compliment."

"You should, you don't seem to have many admirable characteristics but you do have some useful ones like your connection with, what is it they call you, ah yes, wise guys. But it is what it is. Tell me about Giancana."

Gino gave her the Reader's Digest history of Giancana and the Chicago 'Outfit.'

"So let me see if I understand. Giancana became the boss but these other guys, Accardo and Ricca still kept control?"

"Yeah, that's right. And don't forget the CIA connection. Between that and his ties to the Kennedy's you really think he's worth saving?"

Maggie shrugged. "Not for me to decide. I'm in field operations not admin."

"Christ, you even have bureaucracies in heaven?"

"Who do you think created them? And Christ is not..."

Gino chuckled. "Yeah, yeah, I know. Not involved. Anyway, how about we help Sam finish off Castro? That might give the CIA a reason to leave him alone."

"My instructions are to keep this domestic, no foreign intrigue."

"Okay, then we need to get to Oak Park, Illinois a week or so before June 19, 1975, to give us some time to work with."

"Is that the date he was killed?"

"Yup."

"Hmm, how about we try something different? You said the CIA killed him to stop him from testifying before the Senate about their involvement. Let's go right to the source and derail the CIA before they ever contact them."

"And how are we supposed to do that? It's not like there were pictures of the meeting. They tend to keep that stuff quiet."

"How about we run a little interference on Maheu and Exner? Stop them and we stop what they put in motion."

"How is it you know about them and not the CIA?"

"Google, of course. We have our own version of the algorithm. A better one since it is infallible." She smiled, waiting for his answer.

"Well, Maheu is an interesting character. I never bought the story he scammed Giancana and Santo Trafficante with his cover story. They knew someone in the government sent him. But in this business if you have the right amount of money you can buy a bullet in the head for anyone."

"That's a lovely thought," Maggie said. "Everyone's life has a price tag."

"Yeah well, you knew what you were dealing with when you guys gave me this gig. But like I told JB, if there is one weakness these guys all share it is they trust no one.

"Show'em the money and they'll handle the job. But they do it in a way so if you did decide to rat 'em out it will be your word against theirs and you won't make it to court. They'll put one in your head for free."

Maggie shook her head. "Look what I've become, sitting in a bar discussing a how-to-take-out-rats and arranging murders scheme with a mob boss. I don't recall signing up for this."

Gino chuckled. "No worries, Maggie, you get used to it after a while and good at it."

She glanced up at him. “Said the guy with bullet holes in the back of his head.”

Gino involuntarily rubbed his head. “True, and it proves my point. These guys have vulnerabilities we can exploit. And doubt and mistrust are the two most powerful.”

Gino downed his drink. “Come on, let’s go. We need a few things before we go meet Maheu and Exner. A hotel room and some different clothes.”

“Why Exner? Isn’t Maheu enough?”

“Nothing convinces a wise guy of treachery better than having two separate sources spreading it. Especially if they don’t know each other. Trust me, between Maheu on one side and Exner adding pillow talk, Sammy will run from these guys.”

“Or kill’em.” Maggie added.

Chapter XIX Realities

"So tell me again why we need to dress like this?" Maggie said, a bit uncomfortable in the less than stylish plain red dress. The mirror in the hotel bathroom didn't help.

Gino adjusted his hat as he admired himself in the mirror. The off-the-rack suit, a bit undersized, was nothing like the custom suits he had made in New York. But this was the effect he was going for.

"Because every FBI agent I ever met had the fashion sense of a colorblind high school junior. And they all wore these stupid hats because J. Edgar liked it that way. Who by the way probably had a dress like that in his wardrobe."

"I didn't think the FBI had any female agents then." Maggie said.

"They'd just started in 1972. The only reason I know this is I had a court clerk on my payroll. He kept tabs on the US

Attorney's office for me and gave me a heads ups. Told me to be careful who I talked to at bars."

"Did it work?"

"Well, they never arrested me so I guess it did. Now, time for you to work your magic. We need to get to Maheu's office in D.C. Do you think you can handle that for us?"

In a flash, they found themselves in front of a tall office building a short distance from the White House.

"I take it this is Maheu's office?" Maggie said.

"Yup, and if I am not mistaken there is the man himself." Gino pointed to a well-dressed, balding man carrying a brief case as he walked toward the main door. To anyone passing by unfamiliar with the name Maheu, he would seem just another D.C. lobbyist with a case full of money and a list of favors to be purchased from Senators and other governments.

"He doesn't look very nefarious to me." Maggie said. "He's a spy?"

"More a freelance contractor for the CIA and FBI. They used him for "cut-out" missions—operations for which the agencies could have no direct involvement for logistical and legal reasons.

"Like we would bring in shooters from outside for a hit. Unfamiliar faces rarely arouse suspicion."

"That's such a lovely business practice," Maggie said, "I will never understand why we pick people like you for these things."

Gino chuckled. "JB said the same thing. Anyway, don't underestimate this guy. He was an intelligence officer in the OSS—the precursor to the CIA—during World War II, Now he works as the lawyer for Howard Hughes, the reclusive millionaire, and makes himself a substantial living managing Hughes businesses.

"I heard they based the TV show *Mission: Impossible* on his life. But who knows? We need to be cautious with this one."

"Why would anyone want to watch a show about a guy like him?"

Gino rubbed his forehead. "You don't get out much, do you? I'll give you an insight into humans. Bad people do what good people dream. That's all you need to know. Now let me think a bit, and I think best with a scotch in my hand."

Maheu was the real deal and not one easily fooled. Gino knew to approach guys like Maheu it would take more than a fast-talking former mob boss and a pretty faced woman.

Deception was second nature to guys like Maheu and his natural proclivity for self-preservation would only enhance his paranoia around new faces. What they needed was someone, or something, familiar to bridge the gap and give Maheu a reason to talk with them.

Chapter XX Beware Anyone Bearing Gifts

"So what's the rule about breaking the law again?"

"That depends, I suppose," Maggie said. "What do you have in mind?"

"Nothing too dramatic. A little failed assassination attempt."

"Failed?"

"Yeah, we go to Maheu. Tell him we're from a clandestine unit with the Bureau and have info the CIA is going to have him eliminated. He won't buy it but will play along until he checks with his contacts.

"They'll deny it of course. Then, when he goes home we pop a few rounds at him, missing of course. Then, he'll think his contacts are in on it. Nothing like paranoia to create opportunity."

"I don't know, this sounds a bit risky."

"Everything we're doing here is risky," Gino said. "Look, you got me because I know how these guys work. Believe me, nothing says you're dead man walking like a few bullets zipping past your ears."

Maggie stayed quiet for a moment. "Okay, but on one condition."

"What's that?"

"I pull the trigger. I don't want you going, oops didn't mean to kill him."

Gino stared for a long moment. "Have you ever fired a gun?"

"No, but if you can do it how hard can it be?"

Gino chuckled. "You know, you're right. Pulling the trigger is easy, killing someone is the hard part."

"Wow," Maggie said, "will wonders never cease. You do have some empathy inside you, don't you?"

"Look, I may have taken out a few guys in my day, but that doesn't mean I liked it. Some of those guys had kids and a wife. Don't get me wrong, they knew the game and the rules, but it didn't make it any easier."

This unexpected human side of Gino gave Maggie pause, but she quickly got over it. "You still pulled the trigger. You didn't have to do that."

"I did pull the trigger," Gino said, his eyes narrowing. "And that is why I am here, so deal with it."

Maggie held his gaze for a moment. "Let's just do this and be done with it, okay?"

Gino held up his hands. "Okay, okay. Just follow my lead." He started across the street toward the office. As they got to the sidewalk, a car pulled up in front of the office. Two men in suits got out and went inside.

"Hang on," Gino said. "those two suits are definitely agents. Probably the Bureau but could be CIA." Rubbing his hand over his mouth he thought for a moment. "We can use this. Can you create a bit of a disturbance when they come out? Nothing too big, just draw their attention a bit."

"Sure," Maggie said. "Tell me when."

They found themselves a spot to watch the front door. Twenty minutes later, the two agents left the building, Gino pushed Maggie toward them.

"Excuse me, sir," Maggie said, "do you know if this is the law office for John Schultz?" The smile dazzled the men.

"No, sorry. I never heard of him," one said, "how about you, Tim?"

"Nope, don't know him. You sure this is the address?"

Maggie made a production by looking through her pocketbook. "I had it here somewhere."

"Can I help," Gino said, pushing his way between the two men.

"Do you know where Attorney John Schultz's office is?"

"I would hope so, "Gino smiled. "I'm John Schultz."

"You are?" Maggie said. "Oh, great. Thanks, gentlemen, all set now."

Gino and Maggie headed toward the door, leaving the two agents watching as they walked away. Once inside, Gino pulled her away from the door.

"Hang on, let them leave first." Watching the agents drive away, Gino motioned toward the coffee shop in the lobby. Finding a table, they ordered coffee and sat down.

"So what did that accomplish? You like pretending to be a lawyer?"

Gino smiled, reaching into his jacket pocket. Out came two leather ID cases embossed with the FBI logo and containing the ID cards and FBI badges.

"Oh my God, you stole their IDs?"

"let's just say I borrowed them."

"But if Maheu is as good, and paranoid, as you say he either will remember them or look at the pictures and know it isn't us."

“Not once have I finished doctoring them a bit. These things are a piece of cake. You’d think an agency like the bureau would make it a challenge.”

“You can’t be serious. You’ll never pull it off.” Maggie said, shaking her head.

“You mean unlike the last time when we grabbed that rat in witness protection right out of their hands and... well, let’s just say this won’t be my first time. It will work, trust me.”

“Trust you? Trust a guy who just admitted kidnapping a witness and who knows what else you did. Why would I trust you?”

“Because this is how we get to Maheu and I have a track record of success. I’m not asking you to admire what I’ve done—although I am not admitting anything—just accept the fact I can do this. Let’s go find somewhere where I can work.” Gino started down the street.

“Oh, yeah, and we need pictures taken. Find a photo studio will ya.”

Two hours later, the emerged from the central library, expertly altered FBI credentials in hand.

"Very helpful librarians here. Most accommodating with glue and scissors," Gino said.

"When this is over, I am requesting a transfer back. This cloak and dagger is not for me. JB I better suited."

"Come on, Maggie. When was the last time you had this much fun? From what I've seen it was a bit boing up there," Gino said, pointing toward the sky.

"Whatever, let's just do this."

It was a short walk back to Maheu's office. They arrived in time just in time to see him walking out the front door.

Gino made his way through others on the sidewalk and caught up to Maheu. Maggie followed right behind him.

Maheu turned as if he sensed Gino's presence. Sizing him and Maggie up he took a step toward them.

"Twice in one day? Why the sudden interest from the Bureau?"

Maheu had made one of the fatal mistakes of existence, he assumed he was better than he really was.

Gino reached into his pocket and produced the ID. "Just to be sure, no?" Gino said.

Maheu gave the ID a once over, then looked at Maggie. "So Edgar took the leash off the women for the moment and let them out on the street I see." He held his hand out for her credentials.

Glancing between the ID holder and Maggie, he closed it then went to hand it back. Just before she took it, he pulled it back. "Who signed the ID and on what date?"

Maggie held his gaze, then smiled. "Acting FBI Director L Patrick Grey on January 23, 1973. Right in the middle of the Watergate affair."

Maheu smiled, then handed her the holder.

"Alright," he sighed. "What can I do for you now? I thought I was clear with the other two agents I want no part of this."

Gino glanced around making sure no one was within earshot. "That's the thing, Mr. Maheu. They weren't agents. At least not on any Bureau roster. They've either gone rogue or they're from another alphabet soup agency if you get my drift."

"And this matters why? I said I wasn't interested."

"Because they gave you enough info to figure out the target. And they don't want any loose ends."

Maheu glanced at Maggie, then back at Gino.

"And you know this because... never mind. I know my office is bugged. I told the that when they showed up." He paused for a moment, the fear, uncertainty, and doubt beginning to bubble to the surface.

"Anything else?" he asked, waiting for Gino to answer.

Gino looked at Maggie. "Do we go all in?"

She nodded.

"Look, we were sent here just to give you a heads up about those agents. And I'm only guessing at this, but I think my bosses know something they are not sharing and it may involve somebody wanting to take you out."

Maheu laughed, but with a tinge of nervousness about it. "Well, look. Thanks for the info. I can handle myself well enough without your help. Take care." He switched the briefcase to his left hand, patting his right side with his right hand.

Making sure the gun was ready to go no doubt, Gino thought. But i got him wondering.

Gino took out a pen and wrote down a number. "This is a private line to my desk. Call me if you need anything, okay?"

Maheu took the paper and stuck it in his pocket. "Thanks, but I wouldn't sit by waiting for the call. Take care."

Gino and Maggie watched him walk down the street.

“So what happens if he calls that number? He’ll know this is bullshit.”

“it’s the number to the room I rented at the Biltmore. That’s why I went with the penthouse, comes with a private unlisted number. Once we pop a couple of rounds at him, he’ll call. He’d worry about calling anybody else. Uncertainty and doubt are powerful weapons.”

“What if he has one of his contacts look up the number first? I don’ think an unlisted number is much of a problem for these guys.”

“Then we will go to plan B.”

“Plan B?”

“Yup, hit him next time we shoot at him.” Gino smiled. “Just kidding. Trust me, he’ll call. Right now he thinks the number is useless. Couple of rounds zipping by him will change that.”

Chapter XXI Hiding in Plain Sight

"I'm not sure about this, Gino. It's a bit outside the rules." Maggie said, trying to adjust to the too tight dress with the plunging neckline.

"Look, I'm not supposed to go back to my old habits. This is the best I can do without that. These guys, and girls, don't play by rules. Just go in there, sit down next to her and try to talk to her. I'll come in later. You just play along."

"You sure this will work?

"I'm certain a woman who is dating a mob boss and dated the President of the United States will be very interested in hearing our conversation. Just keep it to general topics until I get there."

"Okay, here it goes." Maggie walked toward the front door. Gino couldn't help admiring the view from his perspective. Maggie was quite a looker given the circumstances. Gino wondered if his charm had worn her down. He wasn't in the mood for losing body parts right now. If heaven was anything as promised, he might need all is parts to enjoy paradise.

Once Maggie's eyes adjusted to the dim lights, she spotted Judy Exner at the bar. A creature of habit, this was her afternoon spot. She'd wait and see who of her competing lovers would send for her first.

A girl's gotta do, I guess, Maggie thought, walking to the bar. "Anyone sitting here?" she asked the bartender.

"Nope, all yours," he said. "What'll you have?"

She sat in the seat one over from Judy. "Martini, straight up, two olives, extra dry."

The order caught Judy's ear. "A kindred soul I see. Appreciates a proper drink." She hoisted her glass, tipping it to Maggie.

"My father taught me to like them that way. It reminds me of him." Maggie said, surprising herself with her comfort in lying to the woman.

"He's passed?" Judy said.

"Yup, five years now. I miss him every day."

Judy turned to face her. "Judy Exner," she said, extending her hand.

"Maggie, Maggie O'Rourke," taking the hand.

"So what brings you to drinking at two in the afternoon?" Judy asked.

"Men, of course, what else could it be," Maggie chuckled, reaching for the drink.

"I could have guessed. You live in DC?"

"Nah, just came to visit a friend and he stood me up."

"Typical," Judy said, shaking her head.

Judy finished her drink, ordering another. "Can I buy you one? Help drown the anger?"

"Sure, why not." Maggie laughed, finishing hers as well.

As the bartender put the drinks up, the door opened. Gino, now dressed like he had returned to his old life made his way to the bar.

"Hi, Mags, I'm sorry. I know no excuse but it couldn't be helped. I had to catch a later flight out of Chicago."

Maggie hesitated a moment. "Why, I thought we had plans? Why am I always the one that has to get kicked to the curb because your boss needs help?"

"I know, we did. But you know how he is," Gino glanced around. "That Roselli thing has been stirring up shit and we had to deal with it." Out of the corner of his eye he could see the names had caught someone's ear.

"Look, I'll make it up to you. Tonight, dinner wherever you want. I just have to go make a few calls. I'll be right back." Gino tossed a hundred-dollar bill on the bar. "Keep the drinks coming and have your best Scotch, neat, waiting for me when I get back."

Gino winked at Maggie and headed toward the payphone.

Maggie looked at the bartender. "Well you heard what he said. Bring my friend and I another round. And don't worry about anything. That hundred has a bunch of cousins in my boyfriend's pocket," she winked at the bartender. "Know what I mean."

"I certainly do," the bartender said, comforted by knowing he'd made his tips for the night with just these three.

"Can I ask you something, Maggie?" Judy said. "I couldn't help overhearing the… "

Maggie laughed, cutting her off. "Who are you kidding? We all listen in on those conversations. I would have if it was you and your boyfriend." She paused a moment. "You have a boyfriend, right?" She glanced down at Judy's hand. "I don't see a ring and you don't look like a hooker."

Judy laughed out loud. "No, not a hooker and I do have a boyfriend, of sorts. That's the thing," she glanced around then leaned in. "The guy I'm seeing is Sam Giancana and I know the name Roselli. Sam thinks some guy named Santo is out to get them."

She paused a moment to take a drink. "Probably shouldn't be saying this but if you guys are involved with them you better be careful. There are CIA guys involved. They went after another friend of mine and I think they killed him."

"Who?" Maggie asked, "What friend?"

"Let's just say you'd know the name, but I'd rather not bring it up. Sam is coming here to meet me for a few days. Maybe we can all get together since you boyfriend knows him."

Maggie started to panic but got herself under control. "Yeah, ah, that would be great. I'd have to ask Gino, he's all over the place. I never know when he'll be taking off or coming back."

"And here I am," Gino said, looking to the bartender for his drink that appeared as if by magic. Nothing motivates service like money, Gino thought. "What do you want to ask me?

"Well, Judy here thought we'd like to get together with her and Sam." She turned her head away from Judy so only Gino could see her eyes opening wide in a silent plea for help.

"That would be great!" Gino said.

"It would?" Maggie said. "I mean, yeah, of course. It would be great." Giving another wide-eyed plea to Gino.

"When were you meeting him?" Gino asked.

"Later tonight, around 6, maybe," Judy said. "He's coming here to pick me up."

"Tonight? Ah, tonight won't work. We've got plans and I can't change them. Is he here for just the night or longer?"

Judy shrugged, sipping her drink. "I'm not privy to the schedule. I just answer the summons." She paused a moment, then looked at Maggie. "You know, maybe you were wrong and I am a hooker."

"Oh, Judy of course you aren't," Maggie said, reaching over and patting her hand.

"Yeah, well, to answer your question, Gino, Sam will be, or says he will be, here sometime around 6 and we will be having dinner. After that, I have no idea." She drained the drink and pushed it to the inside edge of the bar.

"Fill 'em up," Gino said, nodding at the bartender.

Once the drinks arrived, Gino moved between Maggie and Judy. "Okay, look. I'm not gonna play around anymore, Judy," raising his head a looking around the bar. "I don't work for Sam."

Judy pulled back a bit, giving a side glance at Maggie.

"Maggie here is as she seems, pretty to look at but clueless. She runs in circles with the kind of guys as Sam and is useful to us." Whispering so Maggie wasn't part of the conversation.

"You're a cop?" Judy said, pulling way back.

"Not quite. FBI and if you want to keep seeing Sam you'll listen to what I have to say."

"I don't think so," Judy said, pushing the drink away. "I'm outta here."

"Okay, but you might not want to sit too close to Sam. He's a marked man."

Judy spun in her seat. "What's that supposed to mean?"

"I'm gonna keep this simple. You do whatever you want with it. Sam and your friend Maheu have a problem."

At the sound of Maheu's name Judy's face changed. She paled a bit, then blinked a few times. Gino knew he had her attention now.

"Yeah, that's right. We know all about the connection between you three. Let's just say your past is catching up with you. There's nobody left in high places to protect you. You think Sammy's coming here to see you? Not likely.

"He's coming here because Maheu sent him a message. They need to talk. We know there's a hit out on both of them. Could be the wise guys. Could be our black sheep cousins in the CIA. Or it could be a powerful political family that prefers to keep their secrets and indiscretions out of the public view. But whoever it is, it won't end well for any of you."

Judy remained quiet for a long moment, her gaze focusing on a distant wall. "This is bullshit. More FBI bullshit to get to Sam. Or you're with some other organization playing a part. How do I even know you are FBI?"

Gino produced the FBI ID case. "Go ahead, call the FBI office and ask for me. Leave a message because I'm not in."

Judy looked at the ID then tossed it on the bar. "I need another drink."

"And the American taxpayers are buying," Gino said, ordering the round. "I'll be right back," starting toward the payphone. "Gotta call the office and check for messages." A smile crossed his face and he winked.

"You didn't know?" Judy said, looking to Maggie for help.

"No, I thought he was just a nice guy. He seemed like the real thing. If they find out I've been seeing an FBI agent… oh my God they'll, they'll… "

Judy reached over and took her hand.

"What did you tell him?"

"Nothing, I don't know anything except. Ah, Listen, I gotta go make a call. I'll be right back."

"Want me to come with you? He's at the phone now."

"No, stay here and make sure he doesn't leave. I'll be right back," she winked. "I know the manager here, he'll let me use the office phone."

Maggie walked around the bar and disappeared. She made her way to the hall and motioned for Gino to come over.

"What am I supposed to do now. She thinks we're allies or something."

"Perfect, play it slow but tell her you heard something about a hit being planned. You don't know who but you thought I was the hitman."

"This is not me, you know. She'll know I'm lying. My voice is shaking."

"Even better. She'll buy it because she thinks you're terrified. A terrified bimbo. Just give her enough so when I come back she'll believe Sam is the target and I'm not who I say I am."

Maggie shook her head.

"Go," Gino said, pushing her toward the bar, "before she comes looking."

Maggie made her way back and sat down, taking a long drink.

"So, what did you find out?"

“From the call, nothing. But I started thinking about something I overheard the other day. Gino was talking to some bald guy, an attorney I think, named Bob or Robert Mathews or something like that.

“The guy said he wanted no part of taking the guy out then left. Gino was pissed. He got on the phone and told somebody we need a different doctor for Sam.”

“Doctor? Yeah right. A doctor with a gun.” Judy went silent for a moment. “I think this guy is bullshit. He’s not FBI. I bet he’s CIA or some other government agency no one’s ever heard of. A friend who would know warned me about guys like this. They’re hard to tell apart from the bad guys because they’re worse.

“I bet he’s trying to use me to get to Sam and you were the bait to get me talking,” she sat back a bit. “Which of course like an idiot I did. I need to warn Sam. Let me ask you something, was the guy he met named Maheu, not Mathews?”

Maggie faked surprise as best she could. “Yeah, that’s it. Ah, I think.”

“Now I know what this is. The CIA is going after Sam because of the Castro thing.”

“What?” Maggie said, growing more comfortable with the feigned ignorance.

“Never mind, long story. I’m gonna call Sam’s driver, he’ll know how to get in touch. You think the manager will let me use the phone too?”

“Oh, ah, he can’t he just left. Sorry,” Maggie said, surprising herself with the ease of deceiving the woman.

“Okay, I’ll wait ‘til Gino, or whatever his real name is, comes back then I’ll make the call. Keep this between us. Okay? My guess is they won’t do anything here in DC, they’re fishing to see when he’ll be back in Chicago.”

Gino came back. “So, I tried to change the plans for tonight but can’t. Maybe another time. When will you and

Sam be back in Chicago?" He smirked. "Unless the invite is cancelled."

Judy gave Maggie a raised eyebrow then said, "Oh it's cancelled. I'm not sure how Sam will react to an FBI agent talking to me, but I know he won't be talking to you or anybody. I'll be right back."

As Judy walked away, Gino looked at Maggie. "So?"

"You got her thinking. She has no idea who or what you are but she is going to warn Sam."

"Okay, finish your drink we have one more thing to do today."

"What, this isn't enough?"

"Nope, we have to go shoot at someone. We'll miss of course, but it will cement the story in everyone's mind."

Chapter XXII Oops

Gino and Maggie waited outside the old library building located one block from Maheu's office. Gino paced back and forth, checking both sides of the street.

"Will you stop that!" Maggie said, grabbing his arm. "You are making me nervous."

"Nervous? About what?"

"About this whole mess I am stuck in. Why I decided to do this I will never understand."

"Look, what's the worst thing that happens to you? Nothing. You go back to doing whatever it is angels do when they're not interfering with life here on this planet. Hey, are there other planets you guys go to?" Gino pulled her into an alcove. "Never mind, get ready?"

"Ready for what?"

"You first burglary. Come on," he said, pulling her along.

The security guard stood at the door, sorting through his keys to lock the door. His daily security check once again an exercise in futility. Who'd break into a closed library full of rats and rotting books no one ever read.

Gino pushed Maggie into the old guy, knocking the key chain from his hand.

"Oh my god, "Maggie said, I'm so sorry casting a glare at Gino.

Gino reached down, retrieving the guard's keys then switching them out for the set he'd brought along. "Here you go, pal. Sorry for my friend here, She's had one martini too many today."

"I what?" Maggie said, then just shook her head.

"No problem," the guard smiled. It was probably the most excitement he'd had all day. He smiled at Maggie. "Maybe you should stick to something less powerful." Then sauntered away.

"Yeah, Maggie. Maybe you have a drinking problem." Gino chuckled, waiting for the guard to drive off.

Maggie just glared.

"Okay, okay. Next time I'll be the drunk one. Feel better?"

"No."

Gino shrugged then looked around. "Okay, come on." He tried several keys before finding the right one and, after one more glance around, letting them inside.

"So now what? What if that guard gets to his next stop and realizes the keys are not his? Then what happens?"

Gino smiled.

"And you know this how?" Maggie asked, arms folded against her chest.

"Benjamin Franklins can buy you a lot of information." Gino smiled, rubbing his thumb on his index finger. "And security guards don't make much money."

"He expected us?" Maggie said. "Then why the drunk nonsense?"

Gino shrugged. "A little drama so you wouldn't give us away to the whole world."

Maggie shook her head. "Okay, fine. What do we do now?"

Gino walked over the former front desk, walking behind it. He reached down and pulled out a sheet wrapped around something. Removing the sheet, he pulled out a rifle with a scope.

Maggie's eyes went wide. "Where did that come from?"

"Benjamins can buy more than just information, my dear. And this never-ending supply I find in my pocket comes in handy. I've been meaning to thank you for that."

Maggie shook her head. "Wasn't me."

"Hmm, JB then I suppose. If I see him again I will thank him. Now let's go. Mr. Maheu is a creature of habit when it comes to his making happy hour at McAleer's Irish Pub. Of course, he might miss it today if we don't miss him. Let's go."

With that Gino put two rounds in the rifle, drew back the bolt to chamber one round, made sure the safety was on, then headed up the stairs to the second floor.

Making their way to a window in the corner of the building, Gino pulled back the cardboard covering and gently broke out one of the panes.

"Hey, you're doing damage to a public building, Maggie said. "That's against the law."

Gino just looked at her. "We're about to shoot at somebody and you're worried about vandalism. Wow."

"Yeah, good point," she shrugged, a sheepish grin on her face.

"Go over to that other window," Gino pointed. "You should be able to see him leaving his office. Tell me when he gets to the crosswalk."

Maggie locked eyes for a moment. "Promise me you are not going to hit him."

Gino nodded. "Just gonna scare him. This is a .22 caliber rifle with low power ammo and soft lead tips. Even if I did hit him it would be like a bee sting. Now get over there so we can finish this thing."

Maggie made her way to the window, pulling back a corner of the cardboard covering the glass. She leaned against the wall to give her a better angle on the office entrance.

"Look, I don't know much about guns, but if the CIA or some other agency were trying to kill someone, wouldn't they use a bigger gun?"

"My, my, our little girl is growing up. This is a message, not an actual assassination. He'll get the message that *somebody* is trying to warn him but he won't be sure. It will be enough to put a guy like him off Giancana which is all we want right?"

“Yeah,” Maggie nodded. Then movement caught her eye. “He’s on the way, just left the building.”

“Okay,” Gino said, taking aim at the point where the crosswalk ended at the curb. “Let me know when he starts to cross.”

It only took Maheu twenty seconds to make it to the crosswalk. To Maggie, it seemed like hours. There were several other people there waiting for the cross signal.

“There are a bunch of people near him, maybe we should wait?”

“I won’t hit anybody, I’m good at this you know.” Gino chuckled. “That’s why you hired me.”

Maggie rolled her eyes. “Okay, he moving.”

Gino moved the rifle until Maheu’s head filled the scope sight. Dropping the point of the weapon an inch or so put the crosshairs right on the umbrella Maheu always carried. More for an inconspicuous weapon than weather protection.

Taking a deep breath, Gino exhaled a bit, moved the safety off, slid his finger over the trigger, then watched Maheu drop dead on the street, at least it appeared so since he wasn't moving and there was blood.

"Holy shit, you killed him!" Maggie said.

"It wasn't me," Gino said. "I never fired a round."

Maggie looked back at the commotion on the street and saw several people trying to help Maheu. Within a few moment sirens started in the distance and several uniform police officer swarmed the scene.

Several of the bystanders were pointing at the old library building.

"Let's go," Gino said, taking off the gloves and sliding the weapon behind a table near the window. "Time to go!"

As he turned to go, everything went white and out of focus. When his vision returned, Gino found himself standing on the sidewalk in the midst of the crowd watching the ambulance take Maheu away.

Maggie was nowhere to be seen.

Gino spun around searching the crowd but came up empty. Oh boy, he thought, she's probably telling Achilles to yank me back and send me to hell.

"Not yet," Maggie said, appearing at his side. "Maheu's not dead, it was some kind of a rubber bullet that hit him. Knocked him out and he'll probably have a concussion but he will recover."

Gino blinked a few times. "And you know this how?"

Maggie smiled. "Angel secrets let's go. I think we accomplished what we set out to do. Maheu will get the message."

Gino shook his head. "Why would he? He might think it was just random."

Maggie grinned. "Not with the note I slipped into his pocket. It will be very clear to him this was a warning not an accident.

Gino stood for a moment looking at Maggie. “If I didn’t know better I’d think you were starting to enjoy this.”

“I’m not,” Maggie said, pushing past him. “But if I am stuck here with you we might as well get it done right. Now let’s get out of here.”

They made their way through the crowd and walked a few blocks finding a quiet neighborhood pub for a drink and something to eat.

Chapter XXIII Reflections

The soap opera on the TV kept getting interrupted with news of the "shooting" near the capitol. There was no word on Maheu but at least they didn't say he was dead.

Maggie sat nursing her drink, lost in her thoughts.

Gino, already on his second, pulled his chair closer.

"Don't even try," she said without raising her head, "Or I will tell Achilles to terminate this with extreme prejudice."

Gino put his hands up in submission and slid back.

"Can I ask you something?" Maggie said after a few moments.

"Sure, fire away."

"Did you enjoy your life?"

Gino sat back in the chair and considered the question. It was the only life he'd known, the world of wise guys. He'd seen his father dish out beatings and bundles of cash. He'd overheard the discussions of who needed to get whacked or who was an "earner" making the crew money.

He'd enjoyed the fear in people's eyes when they found out who his father was. Even the cops left him alone to race the streets however he wanted.

He'd seen his mother cry in the dark all alone on those nights his father was away in prison or out with one of his many girlfriends on Friday nights.

He'd seen her all smiles and pearls getting ready for Saturday night at one of the clubs his father controlled. Or bustling around the kitchen getting Sunday dinner ready for the whole family, blood relatives and those bonded by Omerta.

Even though he'd tried to follow a different path in college, *"the life"* drew him in. Did he like it? It didn't matter. It was his destiny and destiny is not a jealous being. It couldn't care less if anyone liked it or not.

It just was.

"It had its moments. It gave me plenty of money and a good life."

"That's not the question. Did you *like* it?"

Gino finished his drink and pointed at the glass for the bartender. "Nah, I didn't like it. But I had no choice so I became good at it. One of my guys used to say, 'If you're gonna be good, be good. If you're gonna be bad, be good at it.'"

Maggie lifted her head. "There's always choices, Gino, always."

"Yeah, well, not for me. You want another?"

"Sure, why not. And can I ask you one more thing?"

Gino shook his head. "Another question about my feelings? Cuz if you haven't figured it out I never really had any."

"No, not that kind of question. But I know that's not true. You did care for someone once. Someone not in the life."

Gino sighed. "I did, but it was a long time ago. And I ain't answering any questions about her, so don't bother."

"No, it's not about her."

"So what's the question?"

"Why did you pick that building? It seems to me you had to go through a lot of effort to just fire a warning shot. Why not just wait for him at his house and do it there?"

Gino smiled. "I'll tell you why, in one word. Irony."

"Irony?" Maggie said, her attention focused.

"Yup. Maheu was part of the assassination plot against Kennedy, at least it seems he was. I thought it would be a bit ironic if I shot him from the window of a library like Oswald shot Kennedy from the Texas Schoolbook Depository building. Not strictly a library, but close enough."

"Irony, "Maggie chuckled, "who would have thought you capable of such complexities."

Gino winked. "Stick around kid, I'm full of surprises."

The sound of breaking news interrupted their conversation. A reporter was on screen outside the hospital where Maheu was being treated.

"We have breaking news. A police officer and a nurse were wounded just moments ago when a gunman tried to gain entrance into the room of the shooting victim, Robert Maheu.

"Officers were able to shoot and kill the suspect but not before he shot the two victims. Both are expected to recover. Earl reports indicate the gunman is a known associate of organized crime. More to follow as it becomes available."

"Looks like our message to Sam was received and he decided to up the ante. But at least he'll keep his head down for a while until the heat is off."

Maggie stared at the screen. "How is this ever going to stop? This is insanity."

"Welcome to my world, Maggie." Gino raised his glass and drained the drink. "And here's to irony."

Chapter XXIV TP-2p.m.-Fox

While Gino sat at the bar, Maggie excused herself to make a call.

“A call?” Gino said. “Who are you gonna call?”

“How do you think I get our next assignment? It would be a bit awkward if the skies opened up, trumpets blaring, and some of my fellow angels stopped by for a drink. Might scare up thoughts of the Rapture and we can’t have that, can we?”

Gino shook his head, watched Maggie leave, then went back to ogling the two women at the end of the bar. Smiling and raising his glass, he sent over a drink.

When Maggie returned, she caught the tail end of the conversation.

“Wife?” Gino laughed out loud. “No, no, she works for me. A bit of a fancy secretary I take out for after work drinks once in a while.”

Maggie hesitated a moment, then something sparked in her mind. A thought unlike anything she'd ever had before. She knew it was wrong but, well, this whole scenario was wrong so what the hell.

"Gino," she said, putting her hand on his. "Great news. I just talked to the hospital and Marie is gonna be just fine,"

"Ah, that's., ah great, Maggie." Gino said, glancing back at the two women.

Maggie smiled and leaned in toward the women, like she was sharing a confidence. "Marie is my sister, Gino's wife, she was in a car accident and things were touch and go for a bit.

"I had to drag Gino away since he's been by her side since it happened. Poor dear. He's almost delirious with worry. I needed to calm him down a bit."

She smiled and took a sip out of her drink.

The two women pushed their drinks away and started toward the door.

One of them stopped and looked at Maggie. "Your brother-in-law has a funny way of being worried about his wife." Then followed her friend outside.

"Was that really necessary? I was just talking to them."

"Sure you were. But we haven't got time for your dalliances. We have a new project."

"Already? Don't we get a break in between?"

"Nope, right back into it. I never heard of this guy so you'll have to help me understand who he is."

"Man," Gino grumbled, "I need to get a union card so I don't have to put up with this nonsense."

"Funny you should say that. Apparently this guy is some union bigwig."

"Oh yeah? Who is it, Jimmy Hoffa?" Gino said, giving her a side glance of disgust.

"How'd you know?" Maggie said, the shock in her eyes said it all.

"Are you freaking kidding me? Jimmy fucking Hoffa? You want me to save Jimmy Hoffa? No one even knows, for sure, who off'd him."

Maggie nodded. "Yup, but you can finish your drink first."

"Thanks," Gino said, raising his glass without even looking at her. "I hear they paint houses," he mumbled shaking his head.

"What?"

"It means…ah never mind. I'm having another one before this next debacle."

Chapter XXV Teamster Pride

James Riddle Hoffa was aptly named, his untimely, but not wholly unexpected death, was indeed a riddle. The body had never been found and the list of suspects ran the gamut from jealous husband to sanctioned mob hit to an extra-legal government termination.

Gino always knew it was a sanctioned hit. The ties to the labor unions were too strong for anyone to take out a guy like Hoffa unless they had permission.

The wiseguys made shit tons of money off no-show union jobs, teamster pension money scams, and loads of stuff disappearing from the back of the truck. No one would interrupt that without a good reason and a blessing from the boss.

It was always about the money with these guys. Somebody wanted more, didn't think they were getting a fair share, or thought Hoffa would take it away.

That was not gonna happen.

Gino relaxed as they drove through the Detroit suburbs arriving at the Machus Red Fox Restaurant. The restaurant, open since 1965, was a popular place and offered convenient anonymity away from the city.

"So why here?" Maggie asked.

Gino handed her a piece of paper, on it he'd written,

TP-2p.m.-Fox

"Is this supposed to mean something?"

"Hoffa's last entry in his calendar. He was meeting two wiseguys, Tony "Tony Pro' Provenzano and Tony 'Tony Jack' Giacalone. Trying to end the feud with them and regain control of the Teamsters.

"These guys were all union members and officials. Back then the mob infiltrated the teamsters at pretty much every level."

"Do all these guys have nicknames?"

Gino laughed. "Yeah, they used to think it kept them anonymous. But it's not too effective if everybody calls you that in public. These guys are wiseguys but it doesn't mean they're very intelligent. Wise is a bit of an oxymoron. But Moron guys wouldn't sound as cool."

Maggie laughed. "So what happened?"

"Hoffa went to the restaurant and waited a while. Then he called his wife and said they never showed up and he was on the way home. That's the last anyone ever heard of Jimmy Hoffa. He was never seen again."

"So why would he meet with these guys?"

"Hoffa was their fair-haired boy until he got too powerful. Odds are somebody in the organization fed evidence to the Feds. Usually talking to the Feds gets you killed unless it serves the good of the family. Ratting out the rivals is just a business technique."

"These guys play to win, I guess?"

"These guys *always* play to win. And if they think they might lose, they change the rules. If you rat me out, you're a dead man. If I rat you out, it's a business plan."

"Seems a bit unfair," Maggie said.

Gino stared at her for a long moment, then just shook his head.

"When Hoffa was convicted, they forgot about him and figured he'd never return. He had a tough time in the can and came out angry and determined.

"He and Provenzano had once been close but had a falling out. When Hoffa tried to get his support to reclaim the Teamster leadership, Provenzano told Hoffa he would pull out his guts and kidnap his grandchildren."

"I don't get why he agreed to meet with this Tony Pro?"

"Because in our business feuds end one of two ways. Somebody gets whacked or, and this happens more than most would imagine, someone sees a way to make more money by settling the feud with a new business arrangement.

"Hoffa thought he was negotiating his way back into controlling the Teamsters, and thus the money. Turns out he was walking into his own death."

"But they never found the body. Maybe he's not dead."

Gino chuckled. "Yeah, and I'm next on the list for head angel. Hoffa's dead. You don't scare a guy if you want him to go away, you kill him."

"So any ideas on how to stop this?"

"I know one way that always works, but I can't use that tried-and-true method."

Maggie shook her head.

"So we have to resort to subterfuge, guile, and deception. Fortunately, I am good at all three." He paused for a moment, giving Maggie a once over.

"What are you doing?"

"Picturing you in a tight-fitting dress, you're the bait again. It worked last time."

"Oh, no. I'm not gonna try to lure Hoffa away from the meeting. No way, not happening."

"Not Hoffa," Gino said. "Tony Pro. Never knew a wiseguy to turn down a pretty lady and a quick exploration of her more alluring parts for a meeting."

"But I thought you said they didn't show up."

"Oh, he was there. So was Tony Jack. They would want to make sure things went the way they wanted. My guess is they were at another place nearby."

"But how does that change anything? Hoffa would still get into the car or however they got him to leave."

"Listen, here's how I would have done this. I'd find a spot nearby and keep the muscle with me until it was time. We know Hoffa waited a while. I bet they wanted him to sweat it out a bit before they grabbed him." Gino scanned the area. Two buildings down, across the street was a small bar.

"There," Gino said, pointing out the bar to Maggie. "I bet they'll wait there until they decide to move on him."

"I still don't see what I'm gonna do. Not that I would do anything with these guys but wouldn't I be just a convenient alibi for them?"

"Wow, my little girl is growing up. Thinking like a wiseguy's main squeeze," Gino smiled. "No, you're going to be a bit more active than that.

"What I'm gonna do is find out where they hang out so we can try to create some uncertainty on their part. What you're gonna do, when we find them, is go in, sit at the bar, and wait for one of them to buy you a drink. Then, after some small talk, you can give'em a little feel if you like."

Maggie punched him in the arm.

"Hey, okay okay, no cheap feel. After a few minutes you tell them you have a message from Raymond."

"Raymond? Raymond who?"

"Don't worry, they'll know who Raymond is. Just tell them Raymond wants it called off for now."

"You really think two stone killers are gonna listen to a woman they've never met and call off a, what do call it, a hit just because I use the name Raymond?"

"Oh, they'll have their doubts. And that is when the cavalry comes in. Me, of course, without a horse but nevertheless a cavalry in spirit."

Chapter XXVI Play to Their Weaknesses

Gino and Maggie headed back to the hotel in Detroit. Checking in, they gathered together in one of the rooms.

On the wall next to a small table in front of the couch was a wall calendar. The pictures for July 1975 showed kids running through a sprinkler, fireworks over an American Flag, and a Detroit Tigers baseball game.

"Okay, today is the 20th. Hoffa's meeting is the 30th so we have ten days to derail this thing. I'm guessing here, but these guys aren't into long range planning.

"I thinking Hoffa believed he didn't need these guys help but would take it if he thought it would propel him back to the top. So I bet they called him with the peace offering."

"But what if you're wrong?"

"Then Jimmy's going bye bye. But I know these guys. If they decided to get rid of Hoffa, they'd use what they had to lure him in. And what they had was an easier path to what Jimmy wanted. He wanted the power that went with the Teamster's Presidency. They could help him win that."

"But I don't understand why he'd trust them?"

"Trust? He ain't trusting them. He thinks he can give them what they want, money. And they can give him what he wants, power. If you think politics makes strange bedfellows you should live in my world for a while."

"You're dead, remember?" Maggie smiled.

"Thanks for pointing that out. But for the moment I am functioning like a living person so here's what we do. We need to find where the two Tonys hang out. I'd rather not wait until the 30th to get things going."

"And how are we gonna do that? Detroit isn't exactly a small village?"

"Look, I know something about the history here. There aren't that many places they'd go to relax. Well, relaxing might be a stretch. Guys who relax in this business don't survive long.

But they'll have a place they control where they can at least pretend to relax. And I'll bet they use the Lesod Club as one of them."

"The Lesod Club? What's that?"

"Oh, you'll love how slick this is. L E S O D. The Lower East Side of Detroit Club. Genius no?"

It was Maggie's turn to shake her head. "if ever there was an argument against intelligent design, people like you are it."

"Hey, hey. I'm reformed remember?"

"Not yet, you're not," she answered. "But aren't you getting ahead of yourself here?

"What if they haven't decided to kill him yet. What if someone else killed him. I show up with some warning from this Raymond guy and they don't even know what I'm talking about."

"Oh, they decided long ago to get rid of him before he got out of prison. What they needed was enough reason to get permission to whack him. They're just waiting to see how it plays out. See if they can get something more out of it before they take him out."

"These are some treacherous bastards, aren't they?"

"Language, Maggie, language. Is that any way for an angel to talk? These guys are treacherous, and dangerous. We need to proceed with caution. Otherwise I might be forced to return to my old ways."

"Et tunc erit terminus sursum in inferno."

"What the hell is that, Latin?"

Maggie raised an eyebrow, a bit caught off-guard. "As a matter of fact, it is."

Gino saw the shock on her face. "Hey, I had five years of Latin in Catholic school before I got kicked out. What does it mean, I'm a little rusty?"

"And then you will end up in hell."

"Wow, you're gonna have to go to Angel reform school after this."

Maggie smirked, then sank into a chair. "Just tell me what's next."

Joe Broadmeadow
Bobby Walason

Chapter XXVII *The Devil You Know*

Maggie sat in the front seat of the car, tugging on the skirt to pull is down. “This thing is not very comfortable, parts of me are hanging out I do not want to hang out.”

“Ah, but that is how lures work. Just make sure you don’t act too interested in them. These guys are, more than anything else, paranoid. If they think you’re an agent or undercover cop, they’ll vacate the premises. And we’ll have to come up with a different plan.”

“Tell me again who this Raymond guy is.”

“Look, it’s not important. Raymond runs New England. He’s respected all over the country. He had his hands in a bunch of labor unions, including the teamsters. They’ll know the name and that’s all that matters.

“You just get them involved in conversation and, when the time is right, spill the name as the guy your boyfriend works for. Let ‘em know I’m coming to meet you. They’ll want to know why Raymond's man is out here and it will spook 'em... I hope."

"You hope? What'd you mean, hope?"

"Look, I'm not gonna kid you here. This can go one of two ways. They'll either want to figure out why I'm here or they'll try to take me out.

"I can see this whole being dead thing as a real advantage in these situations." Gino smiled.

Maggie shook her head, rubbing the bridge of her nose with her thumb and index finger. "If somebody innocent gets hurt here your deal is over and I will personally deliver you to hell." Her eyes flashed both anger and fear.

"Well then, let's not let that happen, shall we? Look," Gino pointed toward the door of the bar. "That's Tony Pro and the guy coming down the street is Tony Jack. Show time."

The two men, followed by several human gorillas, made their way to the entrance of the Lesod Club. The doorman nodded and held the door for them.

One of the gorillas stood next to the door, folded his arms, and leaned against the wall. His head appeared to rotate side to side directly on his shoulders. From here, it looked like he had no neck.

Gino knew the guy's size would let him conceal a full-size machine gun under his jacket. Whatever he carried, and there was no doubt he carried something, it would not be wise to find out.

The two men and the other bodyguards disappeared inside the club. The doorman took up a position opposite the outside muscle and eyed the street.

While the job paid well, at the first sign of a hit or drive by shooting he was out of there. It didn't pay *that* well.

"How'd you know they'd be here?" Maggie asked, fascinated by the scene taking place in front of her.

"Do you really want to know that?"

"No, I suppose not. Are you sure this is a good idea?"

"Well, that depends on your definition of good. Look, go in there. They want pretty women to come in. Why else come here? Just follow the plan, have a drink, drop the name, and I'll take it from there."

"What makes you think they'll let you in?" Maggie asked. "Wouldn't you be competition for the women?"

Gino smiled. "I'll take that as a compliment. Not to worry, I've made my way into these places before. You just play your part and let me play mine."

Maggie glanced at the club, looked back at Gino, then reached to open the car door. "Okay, here it goes," and she got out of the car, tugging on the too short skirt as best she could.

I'm starting to think hell might be easier than this, Gino thought, as he watched her walk across the street, laugh at some idiocy from the doorman, then disappear into the bar.

Gino knew the habits of these guys. This was their go to place to escape business as much as that was possible for wiseguys. They'd be looking to have a few drinks, round up a few stray women if possible, and blow off steam.

Business was not often discussed in such places so Gino would need to tread lightly yet at the same time project enough intimidation to cower them a bit. Even if they wouldn't show it.

Bravado, not brains, was second nature for these guys but the eyes always gave away fear, even if masked by chest pounding and threats wrapped in a shoulder holster.

After twenty minutes, considering the nature of the place and the dirge of other women entering the door, Gino figured the sharks had already surrounded the new face. And while he kind of enjoyed the idea of Maggie being a bit nervous he knew he needed to get in there before she panicked.

Gino got out of the car, then went to the trunk. Reaching in he pulled out the .357 Magnum, put it into the shoulder holster, and made sure the butt of the weapon bulged against his jacket.

It wasn't meant to be subtle. These guys would assume he was packing but better he reinforced the part he played.

He closed the trunk and noticed he'd caught the attention of the outside muscle. The doorman spotted him as well and even from this distance Gino could tell he was trying to decide between running and staying put. With just the slightest of movements he took up a spot a bit behind the muscle head.

Gino chuckled to himself. The doorman might like hanging with the wiseguys but he wasn't prepared to die for them.

Taking a moment to survey the area, just in case he missed something, Gino took slow but deliberate steps across the street.

The muscle head took a step forward, blading his body and ever so slightly sliding his jacket back. The doorman inched further behind him.

As Gino stepped onto the sidewalk he made sure both his hands were visible. A gun battle here wouldn't help anyone. He took a few more steps, then stopped ten feet or so away from the bodyguard.

"I'm here to see your boss. If you have your friend there," motioning toward the doorman peeking from behind, "go ask, you'll find out I already sent a message inside. They'll tell you Raymond sent me."

Gino wasn't sure the name would mean anything to these guys, but it never hurt to try.

"Stay right there," the bigger man said, then motioned for the doorman to go inside.

A moment later he emerged and whispered into the bodyguard's ear. The look on the man's face told Gino Maggie had done her job.

"Okay, you can go in," he took a step forward, "but the piece stays here."

Gino turned around and started to walk away.

"Hey, the boss said you could go in."

Gino stopped and spun around. His quickness forced the bodyguard to take a step back.

"Look, I'm here at the direction of my boss. I don't know you or anybody else inside this place. I don't go anywhere without my piece. You tell your boss to come out here if it makes you feel better but I'm not giving you my gun."

Gino could see the complex decision process was overwhelming the man's mental capabilities. He was accustomed to his size compelling acquiescence, the subtlety in play was lost on him.

After a moment, he moved away from the door. His eyes were locked on Gino and they did not give off any hint of welcome. Nothing more he would like than to pummel Gino into the ground, but it wasn't his call. He could only hope that moment would come soon.

Gino nodded, took a cautious step toward the door with his hands raised, and reached for the door.

Once inside, it took a moment for his eyes to adjust to the dim light. As he suspected Maggie was the center of a Two Tonys Cookie.

The noise of course drew their attention, as well as the two bodyguards sitting at the bar. Great, Gino thought, four to one odds.

He made his way to the bar, waiting for the Tonys to move back a bit, then took a seat next to Maggie.

"Hey, Babe, what're ya drinking?"

"Wine," she said, her voice a bit shaky.

"Okay," Gino said, turning to the bartender, "Can I get a round for the bar? Scotch, neat for me."

The bartender made the slightest glance toward Tony Pro who nodded, then went to work. Gino spun in his seat, back to the bar, and smiled.

"Gino, Gino Suraci. Thanks for taking care of my girl here." He put out his hand.

"Tony Prenvenzano," Tony Pro said, taking Gino's hand. "Nice to meet you."

"Tony Pro, yup I know the name," Gino turned toward Tony two. "And you are Tony Jacks, right."

At the sound of his name the two muscleheads stood up from the bar and moved to surround Gino. He know faced four very violent, very large, and very curious men.

It was an unenviable position. Having had many such encounters with interlopers trying to muscle in on his territory in his previous existence, Gino knew the next few moments would be critical to accomplishing his goal.

He gave a look around, sizing up the enemy. His inclination was to pull the piece, grab Tony Pro around the neck, and put the gun to his head. The others wouldn't have time to react.

But all that would do is create a hostage crisis of no advantage. For all Gino knew, Tony Jacks might *want* Tony Pro taken out and he'd let Gino do it, then kill him.

No, this required a bit of finesse and calm discussion, and breaking his own cardinal rule of *never* giving up his gun. But he had an advantage they would never consider. He was already dead, made the decision a bit less worrisome.

"Look," Gino said, raising his hands away from his body. "If you'd feel better, take my piece. I'm not here to use it on anyone."

Tony Pro nodded at one of the muscle and the man relieved Gino of the weapon.

"Can I finish my drink?" Gino asked.

"Sure," Tony Pro said. "And you can tell me why the fuck you're here and why I shouldn't put you in the ground."

Gino picked up the drink, downed it, then pushed the glass toward the bartender. "Fill it up, even if they kill me you'll get paid," tossing a hundred-dollar bill on the bar.

He turned back to face the men. "Did my friend here mention Raymond?"

"Yeah, so what? Who the fuck is Raymond?" Tony Jacks said. "Means nothin' to me."

"Oh, I know that's not true," Gino said. "Because if you really don't know who Raymond is then I'm talking to a couple of schmucks and wasting my time."

"Who the fuck are you calling a schmuck," Tony Jacks said, taking a step toward Gino. Tony Pro held him back.

Gino never flinched.

"Look, let's dispense with the drama, okay?" Gino said. "I know I'm on your turf. I know you don't take kindly to people on your turf. But this is bigger than all of us. So stop the bullshit about who is Raymond. You know full well who he is.

"I'm here for one reason, to relay a message. Makes no difference to me what you do after I deliver the message but I am going to deliver it. Understand?"

The two Tonys exchanged glances, then motioned for the muscle to go back to their seats. Taking the gun from the one who'd removed it, Tony Pro handed it back to Gino.

"Okay, so what's the message?"

"Raymond wants Hoffa left alone."

The startled look in their eyes said it all. This was a rogue operation. They don't have permission yet to take him out and they can't figure out how we know. Gino knew he had to tread lightly here.

"Who said anything about taking out Hoffa?" Tony Pro asked.

Gino raised his hands. "Remember, I'm just the messenger. I was sent to deliver it and I have."

"Yeah, well I have a message for Raymond," Tony Jacks said. "You tell him this is Detroit. We decide what happens here. Not some fucking guy from Rhode Island."

Gino smiled. "And you said you didn't know Raymond. Yet you know he's from Rhode Island? I didn't tell you that." He turned to Maggie, who'd remained silent and wishing she were invisible the whole time.

"Did you tell him that, babe?"

She shook her head and resumed staring at the wall. Something Gino said kept echoing in her mind "I hear you paint houses." She hoped she didn't see what that really looked like.

"So if I didn't tell you and she didn't tell you, how did ya know?" Gino smiled and grabbed his drink.

"How do we know you're not Hoffa's guy?"

"You don't," Gino said, motioning for another round. "But now that I have your attention maybe you'll listen to what else I have to say."

Chapter XXVIII Fingers Crossed

"Well that went well," Gino said, as they made their way back to the hotel.

"Well? Look, I know there was nothing they could really do to me. But I prefer *not* to be stuck in the middle of a gunfight.

"Why not," Gino laughed, "just think of the look on their faces when they unload on us and nothing happens. They'll be plenty of shit-stained underwear for their wives to clean."

"Not how this is supposed to be done. We have to keep who we are a secret. Unless you want to go to hell. Then, fine, just blast away next time and before the first bullet leaves the barrel you'll find yourself there." Maggie quickened her pace and walked ahead.

Gino ran to keep up. "Okay, okay. I understand that. But you gotta understand how these guys work. They only care about advantages. If killing Hoffa gives them an advantage, they will. If leaving him alone is more to their benefit, they'll leave him alone.

"They play a zero-sum game. As long as they win, however they win, is all that matters to them. They'll wait and see if we add to their success or take something from them. If they thought we were there to do that, they would've been the ones to start blasting away."

Once in the room, Maggie slumped on the bed. Gino lay on the couch. Twenty minutes later, the phone rang.

"And we now have the answer." Gino reached for the phone.

"Yeah, okay, uh huh, sure. Friday at 5:00 Yeah, I'll find it.. We'll be there." Gino hung up the phone.

"So?" Maggie said, swinging her legs over the edge of the bed.

"So we have been summonsed to a meeting with the man who makes the decisions."

"And who is that?"

"Well, most people think its Frank "Funzi" Tieri and he'll probably be they one to show up."

"Most people think? What do you think?" Maggie now leaned a bit forward toward Gino.

"Look, when I was in the business, it paid to know the history behind guys in charge. How they got there and who they killed to get there. Knowing who their enemies might be could come in handy.

"Funzi ran the show during this Hoffa thing, but the real boss was Benny Squint, Phillip Lombardo. He's a legit boss. If he shows up, we struck a nerve. Let's hope he didn't reach out to Raymond to check us out."

"Wait, this Raymond is a real guy?"

"Oh yeah, runs the New England faction, El patron, the Old Man, Raymond L.S. Patriarca. Sr. I knew the guy when I was coming up in the organization. He died before I became a capo. He won't know the name now, but if Benny Squint reached out we might have a problem."

"We might have a problem. Oh, no. No *we* here. You might have a problem; I will just get to go back to what I was doing which was keeping people like you out of my neighborhood."

Gino bowed his head. "I stand corrected. Anyway, if it's gonna end tonight we might as well go out with a bang, pun intended.

"Wanna take a little roll in the hay before we meet our destiny?"

The silence spoke volumes.

"No? Okay, can we at least go grab dinner and drinks?"

Maggie nodded, then went off to change. Gino positioned himself so as to catch a bit of a view in the mirror when the door didn't fully close.

A voice rose from the bathroom. "If you value your vision, you'll divert your gaze. Otherwise, we'll have to find a restaurant that accepts seeing eye dogs."

Gino chuckled, then turned to face the window. I am losing my touch. Dying has tarnished my skills.

When Maggie came out of the bathroom, Gino was on the phone. "Listen, our friend in Providence has some concerns. We're trying to work it out," he went silent as he listened to the other side.

"Yeah, tonight. Whoever shows up will tell us something. Yeah, yeah. I will. Bye." As he put the receiver down, he saw Maggie.

"Oh my you clean up good. You sure you don't want to… "

Maggie held up her hand. "Never gonna happen. Just accept that."

"Never is such a long time," Gino said. "And since I now have forever to try, I might just wear you down."

"You may have forever, but your forever might be a long way from mine, Keep that in mind. Who were you talking to?"

“A guy with ties to Hoffa.”

“Ah, how do you know someone with ties to Hoffa, this is a few years before you went bad.”

“Bad? I’m not bad, I was very good I what I did. But anyway, remember how I told you I knew the history behind these guys? Well, I knew the guys who were with Hoffa and the guys that were glad to have him go missing.

“Couple of names dropped here, couple of incidents mentioned there, and they think I am the real deal from Providence.”

“And what do they do for us?”

“Once we know the power behind this move against Hoffa, we can use them to block the play if needed. It’s like a chess game. Their opening move will tell us their strategy and thinking. We counter the moves as needed. The guy on the phone is just a pawn, we’ll have other more powerful pieces when needed.”

“Chess? I’m impressed.”

"Oh there's more to be impressed than that, but you get my point. Now let's go have dinner and I will impress you some more by reciting Shakespeare."

Gino smiled when he caught that almost interested look in Maggie's eyes. I am wearing her down, he thought. Only a matter of time.

"No it ain't," Maggie's voice echoed in his mind. "You keep forgetting the power I have over you."

Gino chuckled, and without thinking it he knew he was on the right path in his heart. And that was never wrong.

Chapter XXIX The Unexamined Life

Maggie and Gino sat in the car watching the entrance of the restaurant. The place was quiet tonight, not a lot of customers. Located off the main drag in downtown Detroit, it was one of those places someone had to take you. It was not the kind of place people drove by and thought, Hey, let's go here.

Anyone hanging in the area too long would be noticed. Cops, hitmen, or the media wouldn't try anything here.

In other words, it was perfect for a quiet unobserved meeting, or something less pleasant, in a contained environment.

"They're controlling the crowd tonight."

"What'd you mean?" Maggie said.

"Everyone in that place tonight is with them. They are making sure we are outnumbered and they can control what happens."

"What are we gonna do?" Maggie said, glancing between Gino and the restaurant.

"Go have dinner and listen to what they have to say. Remember, the opening move in the match?"

"But doesn't this look like a trap?"

"No, but this tells me a couple of things. First, they believe we're from Providence, otherwise they'd have come looking for us before tonight.

"Second, they're worried that whatever they had planned for Hoffa will be a bigger problem than leaving him alone. That's why they are pulling out all the stops.

"They'll listen to what I have to say. Make some macho noise about outsiders interfering in their business. Wave a gun around maybe for show. Then let us walk out until they decide what to do."

"Wait, we're still going in there?"

"Oh yeah. Did you see the last two to walk in?"

"Yeah, two women."

"Yup, they're gonna keep you busy trying to get something out of you while I meet with whoever is in there."

"Forget it. Tell them I was sick. I'm not comfortable with this deception stuff."

"Sure you are. You can pull this off. Tell you what. Just play the dumb girlfriend part. You know, be yourself."

That got a quick smile replaced by a bit of fear in her eyes. "But what if I say the wrong thing? I might give us away."

"You won't. If they ask about Providence or anything like that tell them you're not from there and we just travel together once in awhile."

"Like a prostitute? I don't think so."

"Maggie, it's not like you *are* a prostitute, you're just playing one. Remember, 'All the world's a stage, and all the men and women just merely players? You'll handle it."

Maggie took a deep breath, let it out slowly, then a strange look came over her face.

"So, we gonna go eat or you gonna just sit in this fuckin' car all damn night?"

Gina laughed out loud. "There you go but tone it down a bit. How 'bout you go for the high-priced call girl act instead of the street corner hooker. I have a reputation to maintain."

Maggie flipped him the bird, smiled, then went back to watching the door.

Gino checked his watch. "Show time. My guess is the main guy won't show until we are inside and in their control. You ready?"

"Of course I am," Maggie said, flipping her hair back and blowing him a kiss. "I am ready for my closeup, Mr. Deville."

"Oh Christ, what have I created? Let's go."

As theyy made their way to the door, Gino spotted the black limo parked near the back of the lot. “Don’t look now but whoever we are meeting is watching us.”

Maggie leaned in, putting her arm through Gino’s. “You mean the limo?”

“Good girl, you’re catching on.”

“Oh you ain’t seen nothin’ yet, baby.” And she gave him a quick kiss on the cheek.

Gino held the door for her and they walked in. The maître d’ greeted them and brought them to a table for four. This caught Gino by surprise. He’d assumed they put them at their own table as far away from the door as possible.

Hmm, Gino thought, the first move was a bit unexpected.

A bottle of wine arrived and the waiter made a production of filling the glasses, allowing Maggie to taste the wine first.

Two other glasses were filled sending the message that they would soon have company. Two minutes later, the door opened and a couple walked in.

The woman, dressed in furs and diamonds, was a bit out of place for the venue but it was all about the show anyway. She was a distraction.

Gino leaned over to Maggie. "I was wrong about those other two women," he tilted his head toward the couple making small talk with the maître 'd. "She's gonna lure you away while me and him talk.

The guy, while well dressed, was a mismatch for the woman, she gave off an air of elegance, he was more street corner deli type.

But Phillip "Benny Squint" Lombardo didn't need to project anything other than what he was. He was one of the most feared men in the Genovese family and the true boss.

His being here, out of his home turf, spoke volumes about the Hoffa matter. This wasn't some power struggle for control of the Teamsters. There was something much bigger afoot.

And Gino knew he was facing a chess master in a deadly game of deception.

Chapter XXX *What's In It for Us?*

Lombardo stood talking with the maître 'd, then made his way to the table. He put out his hand, "Phil Lombardo, and this is my friend, Monica."

Gino stood and shook hands, nodding at the woman. "Gino, Gino Suraci and this is Maggie."

Maggie smiled. "Nice to meet you."

The woman took a seat and reached for the wine. Phil remained standing.

He's waiting to see what I do first, Gino thought. Letting me make the opening move.

"So Phil, you wanna eat first or talk business?"

Phile smiled, then nodded toward the waiter. "Let's eat, we have these lovely ladies at our table. Business can wait."

If there had been anyone in the restaurant for their own casual dinner, the two couples would look like any other group of friends out for dinner.

They laughed, shared two bottles of wine, and made small talk. From a distance the tension between the two men would have been invisible.

But Gino knew everyone in that restaurant watching them was only concerned with one thing, protecting Lombardo and being ready to act on his orders.

Gino caught the subtle nod to Monica.

"Maggie, the back of this place has a great view of the city," she grabbed a bottle off the table. "Let's go finish this out there and let these two talk."

Maggie gave Gino a quick glance, then grabbed her glass. "Good idea, I can use the fresh air."

Gino also noticed one more subtle move. The maître d' and all the staff were suddenly invisible. Nobody wanted to be a witness to any of this.

Lombardo signaled for the bartender, the only one still working, and he brought over two single malts.

"I assume this is more your style than the wine." Lombardo said.

Gino hefted the glass, swirled the scotch to release the aroma, and inhaled deeply before taking sip. The burn was a pleasant one and the peat aroma divine.

"Always, my friend, always," Gino tilted the glass toward Lombardo.

The man let his stare linger a moment, then took a drink of his own. He let the silence drag out a bit.

"But are we friends, Gino? You come here to one of our towns and tell us what we can and cannot do. That is not how friends behave."

Gino matched the man's stare. Playing his own delaying game. "I never told anyone what they could or couldn't do. I just relayed a message from my boss."

"Ah yes, my old friend Raymond," Lombardo said, looking for any reaction from Gino. "It's not like him to send a message like this without letting us know it was on the way." He paused for another sip. "Why is that?"

Gino looked toward the bartender. "Where's your phone?" He would call Lombardo's bluff with one of his own.

The bartender looked to Lombardo for directions.

Gino smiled. "We could call him and ask him but it wouldn't change anything. The message, whether I say it or he does, is the same. Leave Hoffa alone."

Lombardo hesitated a moment, then motioned for the bartender to leave. The man made a graceful, if hasty, exit.

"Why would our friend care about how we deal with Hoffa? The teamsters are ours; we make serious money off them. Hoffa wants to turn back time. All that will do is bring more attention from the Feds.

"Look what happened last time he was in charge. Some good soldiers went to the can because of him poking his finger in the government's eye. We don't need that trouble."

Gino was winging it now. He knew some of the history of the union mob entanglement, but not all the details. He knew the Laborers International Union was rumored to have similar ties, so he used what he had.

"Here's what I was told to tell you. Hoffa made some connection to a Fed. I don't know if it was an FBI agent or an Assistant US Attorney, but apparently the guy is wired right to the top.

"He been feeding us info on investigations, wiretaps, informants, the whole shebang. Our friend does not want to lose this connection."

Gino could see Lombardo's brain working the numbers. What was more valuable? Hoffa buried in the foundation of some new construction or an ear inside the bureau or, even better, the US Attorney's Office.

He could also see rage. Rage that Hoffa was feeding info to someone else. That alone was reason to kill him.

"So what's in it for us? What do we get for leaving the piece of shit alone?"

"Information, what else? There is a rat in your house. Don't know who yet but we will; all we know is the rat is not some lowly member of a crew. He's a capo or someone with authority."

Lombardo shook his head. "No fucking way. Nobody, and I mean nobody, rats in my family. He wouldn't last five minutes without us knowin'."

Gino finished the scotch, looking around to see if the bartender raised his head and would get them another.

Lombard snapped his finger and he appeared at the table with the bottle, refilling the glasses and heading back to his hidey hole.

"Listen, Raymond told me that's exactly what you would say. He said to remind you about Vinnie Teresa."

Lombardo's eyes grew wider at the mention of the name. He quickly regained his composure. "That was Raymond's problem, not mine."

Gino leaned over the table. "You really want me to go back to Raymond and tell him that was his problem not yours? Nobody ran a tighter crew than him, and yet his number three guy became a rat.

"It can happen anywhere to anybody. Wouldn't it make sense to hold onto a source with access to that level in the bureau.? Look at it this way, this source won't last forever. We'll use something he tells us and they'll figure out they have a leak. When that happens, and Hoffa no longer is useful, what would we care about what you do?"

That made the calculations easier for Lombardo. Hoffa alive, if only for the moment, gave him something of value. Putting him down could come later.

"But what about the teamster Presidency? My guys don't want him back. Nobody wants him back."

"Do they want to get indicted and sent up for a twenty-year bid? Who cares what they want, you're the boss, right?"

Lombardo sat back in his chair. Running his finger around the rim of his drink, his mind considered the alternatives.

"Okay, I leave him alone, for now. And I want to know who the rat is. But you tell Raymond this. If this guy crosses me, they'll never find him."

Gino couldn't help but chuckle at the irony.

"You think this funny?" Lombardo glared, sitting up in his chair. Two of the muscle heads, sensing a change in the mood, rose up.

"No, no. Nothing's funny in this business. How about you make the rat disappear instead, let Hoffa serve our purpose until he's no longer useful."

Lombardo relaxed; the two bodyguards sat back down.

"You want another drink?"

"Nah, time to take my friend back to the hotel and make her earn her keep," Gino winked.

Lombardo leaned in, then whispered. "You wanna trade?"

"Trade?" Gino said, eyes a bit wider.

"Yeah, you take Monica, I'll take Maggie. Monica likes this game."

"Hmm, it's tempting. Why don't you ask Maggie? See what she says."

"Monica," Lombardo shouted. "Come on back in."

The women reappeared and took their seats. Lombardo studied Maggie. His look a bit too much for her comfort.

"Monica, you up for a game of switch?"

She smiled at Gino. "Always."

"Switch? What's switch?" Maggie asked.

Gino nodded his head for Lombardo to explain. This was going to be fun.

The look in Maggie's eyes said it all. For once, she was speechless. Gino let her struggle for a bit, then decided she'd had enough.

"Maybe another time, Phil. My girl here has her heart set on a night with her Gino. Right Mags?"

"Yeah, I do. But maybe another time then I can compare things and decide who was the best." She smiled, touched Phil's hand, then stood.

"Come on, Gino. Time for you to show me what you got." And she walked out the door, Gino hot on her heels.

As they drove away, Maggie glared at him.

"Bet you thought that was funny, didn't you? Bet you thought I was gonna freak out or something. Well, I didn't."

Gino laughed. "Well, there was a long moment of silence there. You were shocked."

“Shocked by two male gorillas dividing up the female spoils? Hardly, I was considering the consequences of ending this nonsense right there and then. But I didn’t feel like spending the next few millennia hosting bingo parties in the Catholic section.”

“Catholic section? Heaven is segregated?”

“Not segregated. But we have to match the expectations of the newly arrived. After a while they start to blend. The Jews hold BBQ events with the Muslims, on Fridays believe it or not, and the Catholics join in. Sometimes on Saturdays they have a full pig roast. Just takes some a bit longer to adapt to reality.”

“What reality?”

“Two, actually. Being dead and that everyone really is the same. Nobody has any advantages based on religion. Even the atheists when they get over being wrong, fit in.

“They often brag about how they wasted so much less time in life than the devout.”

"Hmm, sounds interesting."

"Yeah, well you've got a long way to go before you get your stay-out-of-hell card. Now let's talk about tonight. You really think this will stop them?"

"For the moment, but we gotta get Hoffa to play along."

"And how are you gonna do that?"

"That is a work in progress. I'll think of something."

Chapter XXXI A Trojan Horse

"Do you know what Hoffa's middle name is?" Gino asked, rolling the cylinder of the gun as he spoke.

"Will you stop that!" Maggie said, "what do you need a gun for anyway, you can't use it?"

Gino slid the weapon back into its holster. "It's a prop, part of my persona to play the part. And you didn't answer my question."

"What question, Hoffa's middle name? How would I know that? I'd never heard of the man until a few days ago. And it is unlikely, from what I know of him, I would have come across him in my previous assignment."

"Riddle," Gino said.

"What?" Maggie said, arms resting by her side on the bed.

"Riddle. Hoffa's middle name is Riddle. I find that amusing."

"And this matters because?"

"It doesn't, I just thought it was ironic since, if we don't change things, his disappearance will become a riddle many will think about."

"Well then, Ace. Maybe you need to start figuring out how you're gonna fix this rather than playing with a stupid gun." Maggie rose from the bed and began pacing the room.

Gino watched her moving back and forth, all nerves and adrenaline trying to cope with this unfamiliar setting.

"What motivates a guy like Hoffa?" Gino asked, forcing Maggie to stop and look at him.

"Greed, arrogance, brutality, craving power, how should I know?"

"Ah but you do. It is power. Power over others. Power to do whatever you want. Power to change history. Do you think, before he rose to prominence in the teamsters, he was already corrupt and power hungry?"

"Again, how should I know?"

"Are people born evil?"

This gave Maggie pause. She realized he was trying to fashion a solution.

"There are some with serious psychological problems but most go bad through their own volition. Corruption comes from making decisions without regard for the consequences to others. They are solely based on benefit to oneself."

"You mean people like me," Gino said.

"Well, yes. I looked into your background. I know your father was involved in the business but he and your mother did try to insulate you. Your father never pushed you to follow in his footsteps."

Gino chuckled. "My mother would have killed him. She was probably the only person in the world he feared." He slumped a bit in his seat as his eyes glazed over.

"That changed when she died, didn't it?" Maggie said.

Gino remained silent for a moment. “Everything did. I started skipping classes in school, running some small-time gambling books. My father found out and told me if I was gonna live the life I was gonna do it right.

“It all started then.”

“And Lorain, what of her?”

At the mention of her name Gino’s expression changed, a mix of anger and regret. He sat up and stared at Maggie.

“A lifetime ago. It never would have lasted anyway. She hated my father, or at least his business, and never would have tolerated my being involved.”

“Or kept you out of it.” Maggie said, patting his shoulder as she walked by.

“Yeah, well, like I said, a lifetime ago. I’m just trying to get an angle to play with Hoffa… ” Rising from his seat, he added, “or more correctly, an Angel to play.”

“I don’t like the sound of this.”

"Look, I can't use my usual arsenal of tricks. And I know I have to do this without your pixie dust or whatever it is that powers you but that's not to say I can't use your Angelic tendencies to persuade someone about the error of their ways."

"And how would I do that?"

"When Hoffa was in prison, Tony Pro threatened his grandkids, right?"

"Yeah, and now I really don't like the sound of this." Maggie said, leaning against the wall.

"So what if you play the same part you did with the two Tonys and act like their messenger. Only we tell Hoffa they won't go after him but will go after his family."

"And why would he believe that?"

"Because when he shows up at the meeting—and we know the two Tony's have agreed not to send the hit team—then tries to call home we intercept the call. Make him think they've got his wife."

Maggie stared for a moment, gathering her thoughts. "Assuming for the sake of argument we pull this scam off, what does it do for us? Hoffa will just want to get payback even once he realizes it as all bullshit. He'll still want to run the Teamsters. Nothing comes from this but a delay."

"Hmm, my little Angel is starting to grow up," Gino smiled. "And maybe you're right. Let's take a more direct approach. We meet Hoffa at the restaurant. Convince him, somehow, the election is fixed and he's gonna lose."

Maggie shook her head. "You know for someone who was supposedly a bad ass boss you're not very imaginative."

Gino glared at her. "I ran the tightest crew on the East Coast."

"Yeah, right until two mugs put holes in the ship while you drank coffee. Come on, Gino. What did you use to persuade the two Tonys?"

Gino eyes narrowed. "Fear, uncertainty, and doubt."

Maggie nodded. “Exactly. But the fear part wasn’t the most effective. Uncertainty was. You made them uncertain about their course of action. Greed is their main motivator, you made them uncertain about how to best control the money.”

Gino tapped his index finger over his lips, his mind racing with thoughts.

“What you need is to find something to make Hoffa less certain about returning to the Presidency of the Teamsters. He sees that as the best path for a return to power. That’s what you need to change.”

“A Trojan Horse,” Gino said.

“A what?” Maggie asked.

Gino looked at her. “Come on, your friend Achilles never mentioned the Trojan Horse?”

Maggie shook her head. “I never pay attention to him. All he ever talks about is the past. He keeps forgetting he’s dead and the past is ancient history.”

"Okay, listen. The Trojan Horse was a giant wooden statue the Greeks built. They hid Greek soldiers inside and left it at the gates of Troy.

"When the Trojans saw the horse, they thought the Greeks had given up and left it as a tribute to them so they dragged it inside.

"That night, the hidden soldiers snuck out a trap door, opened the gates to the city, and let the returning Greek Army into the city, defeating the Trojans and winning the war."

"So you want Hoffa to build a wooden horse?"

"Figuratively speaking. What we're gonna do is convince him this is the way to keep power in the Teamsters. He avoids jail, mob hits, and threats to his family. All he has to do is use a Trojan Horse.

"He picks someone he can control as President and that person, once he has the power, appoints Hoffa as a senior adviser. A Trojan horse for the 20th century."

Maggie thought it over for a moment. “I don’t know about this. Sounds a bit complicated.”

Suddenly an ethereal voice permeated the room. “It’s brilliant just as I designed it in Troy.”

Maggie shook her head. “Achilles, you said you’d let me handle this. Now your spying on me?”

Achilles appeared in the room, dressed in his former soldierly splendor. “I’m not spying, I’m monitoring your progress. And I’m worried you’ll fail to see the brilliance of the plan.”

“You mean the brilliance of it’s duplicating your idea,” Maggie said,

“That too,” Achilles answered. “Now get on with it. While I am certain *this* episode will end successfully, the track record of our friend here is dismal at best and I have quite the send off planned to condemn him to hell when its time.”

“Hey, I thought I had a chance here?” Gino said.

“Oh, you do, you do,” Achilles answered. “But the window for success is closing rapidly and I for one am certain you will fail.” He held up his hand to stop Gino’s reply.

“I’ll leave you to devise your Trojan Horse and,” turning to Maggie, “I will leave whatever else happens here in your hands, Maggie.”

Achilles began to fade into the mist. “And Maggie.”

“What?” she said, annoyed at the interference.

“I’ve ordered a whole new bingo hall for you…just in case.” And the image faded completely.

“Come on, Mags. Ignore that guy. We’re gonna prove him wrong.

Chapter XXXII A Change of Plans

As the time grew close for the meeting with Hoffa, Maggie grew uncharacteristically quiet.

"Is there something bothering you?" Gino asked.

"What? No, not at all," Maggie said, staring out the window.

"Yes there is. Come on, out with it."

Maggie hesitated, then turned to face him. "It was something Achilles said about being certain you would fail."

"He's just a dick, ah, pardon the expression. You now that." Gino said.

"Oh, he's more than that. It wouldn't be beneath him to, how should I put this, complicate things for you."

'And why would he do that?"

"Because he doesn't like this whole second chance concept. He thinks it's a waste of effort."

"Look, I'm not much for religion, although I may have to reevaluate things, but isn't forgiveness like a big part of your whole gig? Repent ye sinner and all that?"

"It's supposed to be, but like every organization, we have our saboteurs."

"How do they get away with it? I thought your boss was omnipotent." Gino's mind was racing now with doubt.

"Trust. Sometimes trust gets misplaced. Achilles has been around a long time. He has some latitude others do not." Maggie answered, fueling Gino's doubt even more.

"Great, so now I don't only have to worry about pulling this off, I have to worry about being interfered with by a celestial being. Sounds a bit Machiavellian."

"Achilles probably consulted with him." Maggie said.

"Jesus Christ," Gino muttered.

"On, no. He's not..."

"I know, I know," Gino interrupted, "he's not read into this op. So now what."

Maggie shrugged. "I may just be paranoid. He may not do anything to disrupt whatever it is we try to do. Let's just ignore it for now."

"Yeah, you're right. Paranoia is a dangerous thing."

They started out toward the car when everything around them stopped.

"What the hell?" Gino said, looking a bird suspended in mid-air right over his head.

"It's my paranoia come to visit," Maggie said.

In a flash, JB stood next to the car, smiling and waving.

"I'm baaaaack," he said, walking toward them.

"Why?" Maggie asked.

"Change of plans. You're needed for another project who just arrived. You'll enjoy it. It's not a rehab project it's an entertainment tour for the kid's section."

"Really, who is it? Some guy named Moe Howard."

"Moe from the Three Stooges?" Gino asked. "I loved those guys."

"Well apparently so did JC. He's all excited about it and asked for you personally, Maggie."

Maggie was a bit unsure but knew she had little choice. "Can I have a minute with Gino, JB? A private one?"

"Of course, I'll wait in the car. Hey, can I drive?"

"No!" Maggie and Gino said in unrehearsed harmony.

"Okay, okay," JB said, sliding into the back seat, "You can be my driver."

Maggie leaned in and whispered. "Listen, JB is harmless. He's one of the few without any hint of jealousy or ambition but the timing of his arrival is a bit suspect.

"I might have made a mistake talking out loud about my concerns. We know Achilles isn't above eavesdropping. Be careful, my friend. I had my doubts about you in the beginning but I can see there is some good buried in there. You at least deserve a fair chance." She leaned in and gave him a kiss on the cheek.

Gino started to reply but Maggie faded from sight. The world began moving again and Gino was left alone with his thoughts.

The brief respite was interrupted by JB blowing the horn. "Come on, Gino, we have things to do."

Gino shook his head and climbed into the driver's seat. "You don't exactly fit the part Maggie was gonna play I this. I need to think."

JB smiled. "Look, I come with a relaxed set of rules. While I cannot use anything angelic and you still cannot resort to your past practices, we can be a little more, shall we say, direct in our approach."

"What does that mean?" Gino asked.

"Well, if necessary, you can tell Hoffa what was gonna happen if you think it would work."

"Oh, it would work. First, he'd shoot us, or at least try to. Then he'd go after Tony Pro."

"Hmm, I didn't think of that."

Gino sat in silence for a minute, staring out the window.

"Anything?" JB asked.

"Not yet… Do you really want to drive?"

"Yeah!" JB perked up.

"Okay, what do I have to lose? I know you can't kill us but try not to kill anyone else okay?"

"Yes sir."

In a flash, Gino found himself in the back seat and JB at the wheel. He winked at Gino with a sheepish grin. "Let's not mention that little trick, okay?"

"Lips are sealed, now drive."

Chapter XXXIII No Good Deed

Gino was pleasantly surprised at JB's driving. They hadn't hit anyone, just a couple of close calls, but otherwise an uneventful if stressful drive.

Gino had worked out an alternate plan for dealing with Hoffa, but he didn't have much hope. Hoffa wasn't one to be intimidated or threatened, but perhaps he would negotiate a deal.

Arriving at the Machus Red Fox, JB parked the car in the far corner of the lot. The two sat waiting for Hoffa to arrive.

They didn't have long to wait, Hoffa drove in, got out of his car, looked around, then looked at his watch. He settled in leaning against the trunk, eyeing the street.

"JB, stay here for now. I think your desire to drive may have offered me a convenient cover. Hoffa won't know who I am, but he will wonder about why I'm here and who sent me." Gino reached over the seat and put his hand on JB's shoulder. Stay here! Don't try to help me, okay?

"Okay, if you say so."

"I do. Just watch me, okay?"

As soon as Gino opened the door, Hoffa came off the trunk and eyed him.

Gino left his hands down at his side so Hoffa could see he had nothing in them. He made his way slowly toward the wary former Union boss. The prison years attuned him to recognizing threats and there was no better place for a problem than a dark parking lot.

"Jimmy, "Gino said, putting his hands up near his shoulders, "I come with a message and information for you."

Hoffa didn't react at first, glancing around looking for any signs of an ambush. His right hand remained close to his suit jacket.

Whether he had a gun or not didn't matter as long as this unknown and unexpected guy walking toward him believed he had one.

“And who the fuck are you?” Hoffa said in his familiar gravelly voice.

“Gino, Gino Suraci. From Providence. Raymond sent me.”

Gino caught the momentary recognition in Hoffa’s eyes, but the quickly returned to cautious suspicion.

“And why would Raymond send you here?”

“A warning for an old friend.” Gino said. He could sense Hoffa was uncertain if this meant a veiled threat or genuine effort to help him.

“Well, go back to Providence and tell Raymond thanks but I got things under control.”

“You think so, Jimmy? Look, how do you think I knew where to find you?” Gino was adlibbing here, no plan just gut instinct and a long history of dealing with these potentially deadly moments.

Hoffa hesitated a moment, doubt and confusion clouding his face.

“Your friend Tony Pro reached out to a couple of independent contractors in Providence. They were wise enough to run it by Raymond.

“He told them to play along then sent me to give you a head’s up. That’s why Tony Pro and company aren’t here. They were never gonna be here. They were taking you out.”

Hoffa began to rock on his heels a bit. The fear, uncertainty, and doubt fueling an adrenaline rush of options.

“And why should I believe you?”

“Don’t. It doesn't matter to me. I’m just the messenger. You do whatever you think you need to. But just remember, next time Tony Pro my find some talent who won’t be inclined to run it by the boss. They may just take the gig and do the job.”

Gino started to walk away.

“Wait,” Hoffa said. “Maybe I might want to hire some talent.”

"I don't paint houses and Raymond thought you might ask. He said to let him handle this."

"I handle my own problems." Hoffa said, reasserting his forceful persona.

"Like you handled this," Gino said. "Look, I know you don't have a piece under there. No way you'd take the chance on some uniform cop grabbing a headline arrest." Gino looked around, waving his hand, "And you didn't think to bring any muscle so I don't think you *handled* this at all."

Hoffa leaned back on the trunk. "So I'm just supposed to sit back and wait for Tony Pro to take me out?"

"Like I said, Raymond says he'll handle it. Not to be fatalistic but what chance do you have against these guys without Raymond?"

It took a moment for the acceptance to fight its way through the anger, but eventually Hoffa face showed he'd surrendered to reality.

"I want Raymond to call me himself. I need to hear this from him." Hoffa said.

Gino held up his hands. "I will relay the message. But Raymond does what Raymond wants, not what anyone tells him to do."

Hoffa stood at the trunk and watched Gino walk away.

Gino got into the front seat.

"We're not playing chauffeur anymore?" JB asked.

"Nope, we gonna make believe we're leaving then follow him whenever goes just to be sure."

"Oh, boy a surveillance. I've heard about these things."

In his enthusiasm, JB jumped on the accelerator too hard lurching into the street.

A large pickup truck came barreling toward them. JB hit the accelerator harder, but the truck was coming too fast. At the last moment it swerved into the parking lot, careened over several signs, and slammed into Hoffa as he tried to run away.

"Oh fuck," Gino said, jumping from the car as soon a JB pulled over. "Fuck, fuck, fuck!"

Running to where Hoffa once stood, Gino saw just metal wreckage. The wheels on the truck were smoking and spinning as the driver, panicked, tried to pull back.

Suddenly the truck sped backwards then screamed back out of the lot.

Hoffa lay crumbled on the ground. The force of the collision had crushed him under the wheels. There was no helping him now.

Gino started to turn away, then a thought occurred to him. If I'm seeing this, maybe there's something to be done besides leaving him here.

"JB, help me here." Gino yelled, then grabbed the lifeless Hoffa under the arms. JB grabbed his feet.

"Now what?" JB asked.

"Put him in our car."

"And then what?" JB asked, struggling a bit with the stocky Hoffa.

"Ask your friend, Achilles. I think he might have had something to do with this."

"Achilles? He'd never."

'Maggie thought otherwise. Now come on let's get out of here." The noise had aroused the neighborhood and off in the distance sirens approached.

They struggled to get the body into the trunk, then JB headed toward the driver's door.

"Oh no," Gino said, shoving him roughly away. "Your driving license is suspended. Get in."

Glancing in the sideview mirror, Gino could see the red and blue flashing lights. He pulled gently from the curb and headed away, anywhere other than this disaster scene.

Chapter XXXIV You Have What in the Trunk?

Driving for most of the night, neither spoke much. After several hours JB broke the silence.

"So now what?"

"I was hoping you'd have an answer. Can't you bring him back from the dead?" Gino asked.

"No, that's way beyond my pay grade."

"Angels get paid?"

"In a manner of speaking. But either way, nothing I can do."

"What the heck was that?" Gino asked, slowing the car and pulling into an all-night gas station.

"What was…" Then JB heard it.

Thump, thump, thump and a muffled voice.

"Holy shit, he's alive. Hoffa's alive!" Gino said. Jumping from the car and staring at the trunk.

Thump, thump, thump. "Lfft meeffft oufft offft here," came the muffled but clearly angry voice of James Riddle Hoffa.

JB started to giggle.

"You find this funny?"

"Think about it. You're a mob guy with a body in the trunk that is alive. Shouldn't we be finishing him off and digging a hole somewhere?"

"Not the time or place for humor, you idiot. I need the think."

"What's going on," a long-haired, bib overall wearing lanky 20ish kid with a cigarette dangling from his mouth said. "You guys need help with something? You lost?"

Thump, thump, thump.

The kid jumped back a bit. "Wha' the hell's that?"

Gino took a step toward the kid. "Ah, I hit a deer and thought it was dead. Apparently it's not. Is there somewhere around here I can let it go?"

The kid put his hand up, index finger spinning around his head. "Ah, look around. There ain't nothin' until the next town. Let 'em go right here. If it lives great, if not I'll butcher 'em up."

"Thanks, but maybe I should report it to the police. Where's the nearest station?"

The kid scratched his head, then tossed the cigarette to the ground snuffing it out with his boot. "Ah, that it'd be the Sheriff's office on highway 41. But Billy won't be there. He's probably at Good time Mary's for the night."

"Billy? Who's Billy?"

"Ah, the Sheriff. He's the only one out in these parts. But if he's with Mary he won't be much interested in a deer right now. If you get my drift.

"You might find a trooper out there sleeping somewhere, but he'll just tell you the same thing. Let it go. Either the coyotes will get it or one of us will."

"Thanks we'll just keep going for now." Gino answered, ushering JB back to the car.

Thump, thump, thump.

"Sure you don't want some gas? Long road until town."

"Nah, we're good, thanks."

The kid shrugged, lit another cigarette, and shuffled back to the station office.

"You sure you were a mob boss? You seem to be winging it here?" JB said, a bemused smile on his face.

"Shut up or I'll bury you with Jimmy."

Thump, thump, thump.

"You're gonna bury him?"

"No, or yes. I have no idea what I'm gonna d..."

His words were cut off by Achilles appearing in the back seat.

"Ah, I just knew you'd screw this up. I just knew it."

Gino jerked the car to the side of the road. "We didn't screw up anything," he glanced at JB, 'of at least I didn't. Hoffa is still alive although a bit bruised from the experience.

"If your friend here knew how to drive we wouldn't be in this mess."

"Yeah well. Such is life, or death should I say. I have news for you. Hoffa's not alive, he is very much dead. The noises from the trunk were just me having some fun.

"In case you didn't figure this out yet, this is how things were supposed to turn out. We needed Hoffa to disappear and your "men of honor" types have a dismal record when it comes to hiding bodies.

"You fit the bill for what we needed. You see, even though people have free will to do good or evil sometimes what may seem evil is for the greater good. Hoffa's death needed to be a mystery. No one could claim credit so no one would benefit from it. We just put you and your dimwitted friend here in play to make it all seem legit. It all worked out as planned."

"Are you kidding me? This was just a scam? Now what, I go to hell?"

"Well if it were up to me you'd already be there. But I underestimated the influence of that goody-two-shoes Maggie."

"Hey, aren't Angels supposed to be good?" Gino asked, rising to Maggie's defense much to his own surprise.

"We're supposed to be effective, "Achilles said. "Why do you think there are wars, disease, and tragedy? Sometimes these are necessary for the greater good. We allow them to happen because it is sometimes necessary."

"Bullshit," Gino said.

"Yeah, bullshit," echoed JB, then turning away from Achilles' glare.

"Be honest, there are some things you can't do so you use people like me to do your dirty work."

Achilles waved his hand in dismissal. "Let's leave the philosophical discussion for another time. Right now we have to open the trunk."

"And then what?" Gino said.

"And then explain to Mr. Hoffa how he is no longer among the living. I have a feeling he'll react much like you did."

"What happens to him after he realizes he's dead?" JB asked.

"Believe it or not, and I can hardly believe it myself, he is getting the same chance Gino did. A chance to make amends for his many misdeeds. Again, something I argued against but this forgiveness policy has become dominant."

When they opened the trunk, Hoffa came out like banshee, ready to fight. But faced with the startling reality of facing two Angels and Gino against him out in the middle of nowhere he reverted to his instinct to negotiate.

"Dead? Bullshit. How can I talk and move if I'm dead?" Hoffa snarled.

But the bravado faded after both JB and Achilles did the same then reappeared on either side of the man.

Hoffa looked at Gino. "And you, the whole Raymond thing was bullshit? I should've known."

"Well the Raymond part was, but the trying to save you from Tony Pro's hit team wasn't."

Hoffa stared in disbelief. "Yeah, good job on that. I am still fucking dead."

"Yeah, well, Turns out that was out of my control." Gino said, matching Hoffa's stare.

Gino turned to Achilles. "Now what, Ace?"

And in a flash, the entire group found themselves back at the gates of heaven.

Boss Angel

Chapter XXXV An Unexpected Reprieve

Gino, JB, and Maggie stood talking while Achilles introduced Hoffa to his Angel companion, Michael.

“Hey,” Gino said, a spark of his religious upbringing springing to memory. “If I remember correctly isn’t Michael and Archangel? How come Hoffa gets an Archangel and I got JB and Maggie?”

“Hey,” both Maggie and JB said.

“No offense,” Gino countered, ‘but isn’t an Archangel more important?”

Achilles smiled. “It’s just a title, Gino. No offense intended.”

But Gino could hear the sarcasm in the answer.

Hoffa disappeared, leaving the four of them behind.

Maggie walked over to Achilles and engaged in an animated discussion. After what appeared to be an angry response from Achilles, Maggie stood her ground.

“Fine,” Achilles said, now loud enough for all to hear. “This is on you. I want nothing to do with this or any other of your special projects.” Storming off and disappearing through the gates.

Once he was gone, Maggie motioned for JB to come over. She whispered something in his ear. He smiled then hurried off, returning in a flash.

“All set,” he said, a huge grin on his face.

“is there something I need to know?” Gino asked.

“Oh yes there is, my friend, yes there is.

Chapter XXXVI There Are Second Chances

"And I would be alive again?" Gino asked.

JB nodded. "Very much so. But you'd have to stick to our agreement. No more Mister Bad Guy. No going back to the old ways."

"But why? I didn't really accomplish very much."

"Let's just say you impressed us with your efforts. More importantly you won over Maggie. She made this happen. So, do we have a deal?"

"Deal. What *can* I do?"

"Anything you like, just play by the rules."

Gino gave it a bit more thought. "Okay, send away. Wait." He walked over to Maggie. "Thank you, I do appreciate everything you've done."

"Just don't screw this up, okay?" She kissed him again, then faded from view.

As the mists surrounded him, JB's voice, fading and soft, reached out. "Remember, my friend, it's not how long we live but what we do with it that matters."

And just like that, Gino found himself outside the Biltmore. As he took a deep breath and looked around a car pulled up in front of the hotel. None other than Anthony "The Nose" Arrusso got out of the car and walked inside with the young woman, the one he'd sent away with her glass of wine, on his arm. JB had sent him back to just before they killed him.

Gino started toward the door, trying to catch up to the man who'd orchestrated his death. Then a voice caused him to stop.

"Gino?" a woman said.

He stopped dead in his tracks as the voice triggered a flood of memories. The voice from the past that never faded from his memory. Forever young and beautiful. He'd heard it almost every day of his life when he was alone with his thoughts.

"Lorain? My god, it is you."

"How are you, Gino?"

"I'm good, good. How are you? You look, well, amazing."

"I hide the wrinkles and the gray hairs as best I can."

An awkward silence set in. Memories playing on loops in both their brains muted the conversation. The quiet between them interrupted by the appearance of the young woman Gino had seen with her before, back when this whole craziness began.

"Gino, this is my daughter. Angela."

Gino put out his hand. "Nice to meet you, Angela. That was my mother's name."

"Nice to meet you as well. So, how do you two know each other?" Angela asked.

"We went to school together," they both said in unison, a bit too quickly.

Angela's eyes widened a bit as she glanced between the two of them. The silence returned, hanging in the air for a long moment.

"Well, I ah, I should go," Lorain said. "We have an appointment to get to."

"Ah, okay," Gino said. "Well, it was nice meeting you, Angela. And great seeing you again, Lorain."

"You too, Gino," and she surprised Gino with a hug. "Take care." The two then hurried off. As they turned the corner, Angela looked back to see Gino watching them leave.

"So, Mom, the old awkward meeting an old boyfriend moment, eh?" she said with a grin.

"Who said he was an old boyfriend?"

"No one," Angela said, stifling a laugh. "No one had to. It was all over your face. But don't worry, I won't tell Dad."

Gino watched the two leave, then started for the bar again. As he reached for the door, something stopped him. He let the handle go, turned around, and walked away.

And it felt good.

Chapter XXXVII A Change of Hate

He made his way past City Hall, consumed by the deception of nostalgia. Lorain's voice had triggered long buried emotions and he couldn't stop them. The louder they became, the more the tears forced their way to the surface.

Lost in the fog of memory, he never heard the cab driver blow his horn.

The impact knocked him unconscious for a moment. He came to with a crowd of people gathered around. Someone cradled his head, telling him he'd be alright. He never recalled asking the question. Soon, a police officer and several firefighters moved the crowd away and hustled him into a rescue truck.

The rest was a blur until he came to lying in a bed with many tubes and monitors in and around him.

A nurse noticed him watching her and smiled. "So, you've decided to join the party."

"What the hell happened?"

"A cab hit you. The injuries were not too bad, but we admitted you just to be sure. Are you up to filling out some forms? You weren't really in the mood before," she smiled.

"Sure, why not?"

The nurse left and another young woman came into the room carrying an iPad. "How are you feeling, Mr. Suraci?"

"Like I got hit be a cab."

She chuckled. "Sorry, standard opening line. But a sense of humor is a good sign. I'll make this a little less painful." She then launched into a series of questions that seemed interminable.

"Okay, last one. Are you an organ donor?"

"A what?" Gino asked, the pain meds making him a bit slow in the uptake.

"Organ donor. In the event of your death you can agree to donate healthy organs to those in need. It is completely voluntary."

Gino thought for a moment. This was something he'd never considered before. He never really considered death, he'd visited It on others without much thought, but his own death. never gave it a moment's consideration.

"Who would they go to?" Gino asked.

"Well, we would do a DNA test now to see if there are any matches for things like kidney or liver patients you might assist while alive. Then, when you pass, depending on your condition and circumstances, we'd harvest any usable organs for donation to those in need."

Gino considered it for a moment. "Sure, why not. If I'm dead I won't need them."

She turned the iPad toward Gino and he signed the form.

"Thank you so much, Mr. Suraci. I hope you feel better."

Gino smiled, shifting himself in the bed. He let out a bit of a grunt when he felt a sharp pain in his head.

“Something wrong, Mr. Suraci.?”

I don’t know, just felt a bit of a pain in my head. It’s gone now.”

“I’ll get the nurse,” the woman said, and left the room.

Chapter XXXVIII *The Examined Life*

After the nurse had examined him, and the tests ordered by the doctor were completed. Gino had time to replay the events of the last few days or months. He'd lost perspective on time, but he did know this was a second chance.

A few days rest and Gino was ready to go home. One of the nurses came in with his release form.

"Ready to go I bet?" she said.

"Yeah, much as I enjoy the cuisine I need some real food."

The nurse chuckled and started to hand him the form. Her pager interrupted the process.

"Well that is some last-minute timing," she said.

"How's that?" Gino asked.

"There's a match for your kidney."

"Ah, I'm not dead yet. Don't I need it?"

"Well you do have two," she said, smiling. "But I'll let the Doc explain.

A few moments later, a doctor came in. "Good morning, Mr. Suraci. I'm Dr. Charles Burke, a surgeon. I have a very ill patient, a young woman, with serious kidney failure. She'll die without treatment."

"Let me guess, I'm a match?"

"You are indeed. Now, this is not a decision to be taken lightly. There is always a risk to both the donor and the recipient. You can take you time to think it over."

"She'll die without it?" Gino asked.

"Unfortunately, yes. She has a rare blood type so the number of possible donors is very limited. It's a miracle you happened to end up in this hospital."

Gino thought for a moment. Miracle or planning? "Okay, do it."

"You sure Mr. Suraci? You want to take a little time before you decide?" the doctor said, studying Gino's expression.

"What's to consider? I have two good ones and she needs one. I've had a good life so far; she deserves the same. Let's do this. Do I get to meet her?"

"Well, that's up to her. Patient privacy and all. But I will ask."

Chapter XXXIX Altruism is its Own Reward

It took a few moments for the voice to sink in but slowly Gino came to.

"Well there Mr. Suraci, how do you feel?"

Still a bit groggy, Gino shook the cobwebs from his head.

"It's all over?"

"it is," the nurse said. "You did fine."

"And the young woman, I don't even know her name, how's she?"

"So far the kidney is working perfectly. She'll be in the hospital a few weeks or so but it looks good for her."

"Good, I'm glad," Gino said. "When can I leave?"

"Couple of days, there is something the doctor wants to discuss with you."

“Really, that doesn’t sound good,” Gino said, the anxiety fighting against the pain killers.

“Let’s wait for the doctor. She will be here shortly to explain everything.”

“She? I thought the surgeon was Dr. Burke?”

“It was for the organ process. Just relax for now. The doctor will explain.”

“What’s to explain? Why can’t I leave?”

The nurse smiled, that standard I-can’t-tell-you-but-bad-news-is-coming smile and patted his hand. “Just relax. I’ll go get the doctor.”

*****

“Mr. Suraci, my name is Dr. Auger. I’m the chief of oncology.”

“Oncology? I have cancer?”

“Well, sir, there is no good way to tell you this, so I’m just going to explain it as best I can. You have what we call pancreatic afenocarcinoma. If it hadn't been for the surgery, we might never have found it."

Gino only heard the words pancreatic. He could hear the doctor's voice, but none of it was sinking in. All he could think was they sent me back to die.

"So now what?" Gino asked.

"Well, I'm sorry, but the extent of the tumor is such that it is inoperable. We have a variety of medications we can try that may slow the growth or even shrink the tumor, but to be frank, we are not optimistic of success. Do you have family we can contact? A friend, perhaps?"

The sudden realization that after everything he'd done in his life, he was at a loss to think of one person he could call to comfort him. Not one person. He had an army of people who'd once feared him and jumped at his every command, but none he'd consider a friend.

As for family, he'd lost the only chance he had at that years ago. He was alone.

"Nah, there's nobody I can call. But that's okay. I suppose I should ask how long I have left?"

The doctor paused for a moment, looking through his chart. "Let me ask you this: any other health issues?"

Gino tried to figure a way to explain being shot, killed, and reanimated but opted against it.

"Nothing I can think of. Other than I just gave up a kidney. Bit I suppose that doesn't matter now. A few months back I had a bad stomach and back ache. Put me in bed for a bit. I thought it was food poisoning or something. You think it was the cancer?"

"I would hazard a guess it was. You never saw a doctor?"

"Doc, people like me only see people like you when they get hit by a cab."

"I see your sense of humor is still intact."

"Hey, if I can't laugh about it, why bother? So, what do you think? A week, a month, a year?"

"Weeks, I would say, perhaps a couple of months or maybe a little more, depending on the effect of the drugs."

"So no long novels, eh?"

"Afraid not, Mr. Suraci."

"These drugs, I assume they have side effects. I'm not spending my last moments wearing a rag on my head, a diaper, and puking every five minutes.

"To be frank, and I'd like to run a few more tests, but from what I see there are limited options that have any reasonable chance of extending a quality of life."

"So can I leave?"

"We'd like to run a few more tests and set up a schedule for your treatment. Factor in a couple of days to recover from the surgery. We can't start until you regain a bit of strength, but yes, you can go after that."

It took another two hours for the tests to be done, most of that time just waiting for them to do something. The actual process was five minutes. It gave Gino time to think.

What a deal. I work my way back and I get a month or so. And I can't even, no, I don't want to go back to my old ways.

On the way out of the hospital, Gino spotted Lorain crying. Gino wanted to talk to her, but a car pulled up and she drove away. He felt a tap on his shoulder. Turning as best he could in the wheelchair, he saw JB standing there.

"Hey, why are you here?"

"Well, I heard you may rejoin us soon."

"Yeah, thanks for the brief return to life. What you give me, an extra weekend?"

JB shrugged. "That's the thing about life, no guarantees."

"So I noticed." He turned back to watch the car drive away.

"Tragic story there." JB said.

"You know them?" Gino asked, turning the chair to face JB.

"I know of them. When I saw you talking to Lorain, I did a little research."

JB drove Gino home then left him. He wouldn't return for two weeks.

Chapter XL Secrets Cannot Long Be Hidden

Two weeks later, the call came from the hospital. Gino put his cell back in his pocket, then signaled for another drink.

"So, what's the news?" JB said, sliding onto the stool next to him.

"What, you don't already know?"

"Well, I do, but I thought you might enjoy telling me."

"Where've you been, anyway? I haven't seen you since I left the hospital."

"Thought I'd give you some space to live your life as you wanted."

JB sat still for a moment, holding his thoughts to himself.

Gino turned to face him. "What is it you're not telling me?"

"I can't. I'm not allowed."

"Look, it's not like you're giving up any national secrets. I spent the last few months traipsing through time with you and the others. I know you guys exist. So what's the big deal? I'm not asking for the winning lottery numbers."

The look in JB's eyes said it all. No words needed.

"No shit, I'm gonna die. Wow. I already knew that." Gino took a sip of his drink and let the thoughts roil his brain.

"So what was the call you got?" JB asked.

"The family would like to know who the donor is. I have to agree to it.

"So what's the problem? Tell 'em." JB said.

"Do you think they want to know the kidney came from a guy like me? They're better off thinking it was some good guy."

"But you are a good guy, Gino. You've proven that. I think it would be good for you to meet this young woman and see what good you've done."

Gino shook his head and ordered another drink.

"is that a good idea?" JB said, head tilting at the empty glass.

"Why not? It ain't gonna kill me."

"Good point," JB said, "Barman, make my friend's here a double and I'll have the same."

*****

Gino paced back and forth outside the hospital entrance. Unsure of whether to go in or run the other way. JB and Maggie both appeared by his side.

"So what are you waiting for? Get in there and meet this young woman. You saved her life," Maggie said.

Gino listened but uncertainty roiled him. "Only one other time I have ever felt regret in my life but now I regret it all."

"You regret donating your kidney?" JB asked.

"No, I regret being the kind of man who people would not want to have as an organ donor."

"Go inside, Gino. This is something you need to know." JB said, pushing him toward the door. "Trust us on this."

Gino took a hesitant step then timed the entry into the revolving door. As he exited the other side, he stopped dead in his tracks.

There stood Lorain waiting for him.

"Why are you here?" Gino asked. "Is Angela okay?"

The tears came fast and furiously as Lorain hugged him. "She is," she whispered between sobs, "because of you."

Chapter XLI Revelations

"So you knew?" Gino said.

"I knew when the doctor told me there was a donor. I knew it had to be you." Lorain said.

"But why didn't you just ask? I would've done anything for you?"

"We all made mistakes. I should have told you she was your daughter, but I was afraid the life you led would harm her.

"But still I had no right to hide her from you."

"You had every right," Gino said. "It was the right thing to do. Your husband was her father. You have nothing to apologize for."

"Would you like to meet her?" Lorain said. "She knows she wasn't from my husband. And I know she wanted to but never asked about her father. It is time she learned the truth."

"You really think she wants to meet me?" Gino said, holding back as Lorain took him by the hand.

"I know she does. It won't matter one bit to her what you've done in the past. All that matters is you've given her a life with a future."

The walked arm in arm to the room. Lorain's husband was just walking out. "Here's my daughter's hero," he said, putting out his hand. "My name is Tom, and we can't thank you enough."

"I'm no hero," Gino said, shaking the man's hand. "Just happy I could help, Tom."

"Well, get in there. You're all she's talked about all morning." He stepped aside from the door. "I'll go get us some coffee,. How do you like it, Gino?"

"A little coffee with cream and sugar." He tried humor to ease his nerves.

"Coming up. I'll take my time to let you guys talk," and strode off down the hall stopping to thank all the nurses at their station.

"Ready?" Lorain said.

"As I'll ever be," Gino answered and followed her in the room.

Chapter XLII Redemption

"I knew it!," Angela said. "I could just tell. It all made sense. My name being the same as your mother. The look in my mother's eyes when she introduced us. The look in your eyes when you saw me.

"I just knew it was you."

"She's shy I see," Gino chuckled, trying to cover the jumble of nerves.

"How are you, Angela?"

"I'm fine, Dad."

At the sound of the word Gino broke down in tears. "I'm so sorry I couldn't be part of your life. So many times I wondered what if? But I never had the courage to find out."

Angela reached out her hand. "Come here, sit next to me. Look, I'm not saying you could ever replace the man I knew as my father all these years. But the mark of a true father's love is he is willing to risk his own life for his children.

"You did that for me and you never even knew who I was. But I bet if you think about it, deep down inside you knew.

"And now you are a part of my life. Our lives. And that's all that matters."

Gino's heart had never felt such emotion. He was at once furious with himself yet content that he'd had this moment. He'd spend whatever time he had left trying to make up for all those lost moments.

A nurse came in and shooed everyone out. "She needs to rest for a while. You can come back tomorrow."

The words tore at Gino's soul. For him there were few tomorrows remaining and nothing he could do about it.

He waited with Lorain for her husband to return, took the coffee, thanked them for letting him meet Angela, then went looking for JB.

When he'd finished the story, JB was rubbing his own eyes and clearing his throat.

"Angels cry?" Gino said, trying to lighten the mood.

"More often than you can imagine, my friend." JB answered, "More often than you can imagine. Are you okay?"

Gino thought about the turn of events in his life. A young woman, his daughter, a daughter he'd never knew existed, would live because he had done something good for once in his life. It was like a burden lifting from his shoulders.

"I am now, JB, I am now."

JB patted him on the shoulder. "So what do you want to do now? I wrangled special permission to take you anywhere you want for these last few days or weeks."

Gino never hesitated. "You know, JB, I think I will stay right here and get to know my daughter. There is nothing in this world that could ever replace it."

"Okay, my friend," JB said, putting his arm around him. I'll be back when it's time. I've a feeling you and I have many more adventures ahead of us."

“Thanks, JB. You’ll forgive me if I hope the weeks pass slowly. I’ve so much more to live for now.” He paused for a moment, looking at the blue sky as if for the first time.

“Now that I think about it, it’s probably the first time I ever *had* something worth living for in a long, long time.”

About JEBWizard Publishing

JEBWizard Publishing offers a hybrid approach to publishing. By taking a vested interest in your book's success, we put our reputation on the line to create and market a quality publication. We offer a customized solution based on your individual project needs.

Our authors' catalog spans the spectrum of fiction, non-fiction, Young Adult, True Crime, Self-help, and Children's books.

Contact us for submission guidelines at

https://www.jebwizardpublishing.com

Info@jebwizardpublishing.com

Joe.Broadmeadow@jebwizardpublishing.com

Printed in the USA
CPSIA information can be obtained
at www.ICGtesting.com
LVHW011946161123
764164LV00008B/78